The Intrigue

Previous novels by Marion Chesney

The Daughters of Mannerling

The Intrigue
The Banishment

The Poor Relation

Back in Society
Colonel Sandhurst to the Rescue
Sir Philip's Folly
Mrs. Budley Falls from Grace
Miss Tonks Turns to Crime
Lady Fortescue Steps Out

The Travelling Matchmaker

Yvonne Goes to York
Deborah Goes to Dover
Beatrice Goes to Brighton
Penelope Goes to Portsmouth
Belinda Goes to Bath
Emily Goes to Exeter

The School for Manners

Marrying Harriet
Animating Maria
Finessing Clarissa
Enlightening Delilah
Perfecting Fiona
Refining Felicity

A House for the Season

Rainbird's Revenge
The Adventuress
Rake's Progress
The Wicked Godmother
Plain Jane
The Miser of Mayfair

The Six Sisters

Fredrica in Fashion
Diana the Huntress
Daphne
Deidre and Desire
The Taming of Annabelle
Minerva

The Intrigue

Marion Chesney

BEING THE SECOND VOLUME OF
The Daughters of Mannerling

ST. MARTIN'S PRESS
NEW YORK

Library of Congress Cataloging-in-Publication Data

Chesney, Marion.
The intrigue / Marion Chesney.
p. cm. – (Daughters of Mannering: 2nd v.)
ISBN 0-312-13096-1
1. Inheritance and succession–England–History–19th century–Fiction. 2. Young women–England–Fiction. I. Title. II. Series: Chesney, Marion. Daughters of Mannering: 2nd v.
PR6053.H4535I57 1995
823′.914–dc20 95-14710
CIP

First Edition: September 1995

10 9 8 7 6 5 4 3 2 1

This series is dedicated to
Rosemary Barradell with love.

The Intrigue

Chapter One

Nothing is to me more distasteful than that entire complacency and satisfaction which beam in the countenances of a new-married couple.

—CHARLES LAMB

Jessica Beverley felt that the mantle of saviour had fallen on her slim shoulders. After the collapse of her family's fortunes, resulting in the loss of their beloved home, Mannerling, she and her sisters had pinned their hopes on the beauty of the family, the eldest, Isabella. Isabella would marry the new owner of Mannerling, Mr. Judd, the Beverleys would move back to their old home, and all of them would live happily ever after.

But Isabella had fallen in love with their neighbour, Lord Fitzpatrick, and had moved to his other estate in Ireland. Mr. Judd had fallen prey to gambling debts, but unlike their father, Sir William, he had committed suicide rather than retrench.

Hope had come to Mannerling in the shape of Mr. and Mrs. Devers, who had a marriageable son. And Jessica Beverley was determined to marry that son.

Now in her nineteenth year, she rivalled Isabella in beauty. She had thick wavy auburn hair and wide-spaced hazel eyes. But her ambitions received a severe setback. No invitation to Mannerling was forthcoming from the new owners. The Beverleys, when *they* had been rich and wealthy and had Mannerling as their home, had been very haughty and proud, and to a great extent still were, despite their reduced circumstances and their modest residence of Brookfield House. It transpired that the Devers were also haughty and proud. They had heard the local scandal of how Sir William Beverley had tried to get his new son-in-law, Lord Fitzpatrick, to buy back Mannerling for him and how the viscount had refused. So they considered a fellow like Sir William not worthy of their distinguished attention. In the convoluted and Byzantine world of the British aristocracy, it was not necessarily a title that conferred greatness. The Deverses belonged to the untitled aristocracy and could trace their line back to the Normans, something that they frequently did, particularly if the weather was bad and they were confined indoors. Jessica was eager to ingratiate herself with Mr. and Mrs. Devers before the arrival home of their son Harry from the wars, but although she persuaded her mother, Lady Beverley, to send many invitations and presents of fruit and sweetmeats over to Mannerling, curt and condescending notes of thanks were so far the only results.

"It really is too bad," said Jessica to her sisters. They were gathered in the little parlour of their home, Brookfield House. Sitting beside Jessica on the sofa were the twins, Rachel and Abigail. They were very alike, with fair hair and blue eyes. Lying back in an armchair, watching them, was Belinda, quiet and black-haired. Perched on a footstool in front of the fire was the youngest, Lizzie, with red hair and green eyes, not accounted such a beauty as her elder sisters.

"Perhaps you will need to wait until Harry Devers is returned from the wars," said Belinda, "and then perhaps go out riding and accidentally come across him."

"I think it is all very silly and humiliating," protested Lizzie. "Why do we not just forget about the whole sorry business? Mannerling is lost to us." The others looked at her uneasily. Lizzie had always been the one who affirmed that their obsession with Mannerling was a waste of time, and yet it was Lizzie who had tried to throw herself in the river when all hope seemed to have gone.

"It was too bad of Isabella," mourned Belinda. "But she and Lord Fitzpatrick looked so very happy."

Jessica sniffed contemptuously. "Quite sickening, I thought it, mooning around each other in that common way."

"There must be something we can do," said Rachel.

But the days passed, one rainy dark day following the other, and no invitation came from Mannerling.

And then, before Christmas, Sir William fell ill with the typhoid. His illness was short and brutal. He died on Christmas Day.

The Beverley sisters, in the past, had ignored the very existence of servants. In fact, Sir William himself had expected all servants to turn their faces to the wall and pretend to be invisible when he appeared on the scene. The Beverleys had very few servants now and no carriage or horses, but the girls instinctively turned to Barry Wort, the odd man. Barry was a stocky ex-soldier, a staunch presence, a comfort in the dark days. Sir William's former secretary, Mr. Ducket, took leave from his present employ to help the widowed Lady Beverley sort out her husband's affairs.

It transpired that Sir William had actually made a few wise investments before his death on Mr. Ducket's advice, and so Lady Beverley found herself possessed of a reasonable annuity. It would not be enough to let them live in anything approaching luxury, but it meant they could afford a modest carriage and one horse. Perhaps if Lady Beverley had really loved her husband, she might have mourned longer, but for some time she had almost hated him for the loss of Mannerling, hated their reduced circumstances and the very fact that she and the girls had been obliged to have some of their old gowns dyed black instead of buying "proper" mourning. Like her daughters, she was obsessed with Mannerling. She dreamt that, once her daughter had married the heir, she would run the mansion and thus be restored to her former position as mistress of Mannerling.

One day in late spring, she looked out of the window. Barry Wort was digging in the garden, and clustered around him, laughing and joking, were her beautiful daughters. Her face hardened. This was the outside of enough! Her elegant daughters were becoming common and countrified. A governess must be hired as soon as possible to bring them to heel. No wonder they had not been invited to Mannerling, thought Lady Beverley, who always had to have someone else to blame. She sat down at the writing-desk and began to pen an advertisement.

After the advertisement appeared, Lady Beverley was kept busy interviewing governesses. But some were too young, some too "common," some showed the signs of heavy drinking, and so it began to seem to her daughters that she would never be satisfied. Jessica pointed out that they did not need a governess, but her mother replied that they all needed to be re-schooled in graceful manners. Talking to a servant, indeed!

She had almost given up hope when Miss Trumble arrived. Miss Trumble was thin and spare with fine brown eyes, curly brown hair, and a wrinkled face. Her movements were quick and youthful and her voice was light and pleasant. It was hard to realize that she was nearly sixty.

She listened carefully as Lady Beverley droned on about the aristocracy of the family and the loss of Mannerling; but all the while, her intelligent brown eyes roamed about the room, noting the absence of good pictures or ornaments and the shabbiness of the furniture. Then Lady Beverley mentioned the salary in the airy way of a gentlewoman who knows she is offering far too little, and to her amazement and relief Miss Trumble said quietly that she would take the job and start immediately. Trying to mask her relief, for Miss Trumble appeared to be all that was suitable, Lady Beverley asked for references and Miss Trumble said calmly that she would have to have them sent on. All staff, high and low, carried their references about with them. But the thought of interviewing any more candidates made Lady Beverley decide to take a chance, and so Miss Trumble moved in.

As the Beverley sisters were used to talking freely in front of the servants, no matter what rank, Miss Trumble quickly learned all about Mannerling and about Jessica's ambition to marry Harry Devers. Privately Miss Trumble was appalled at the haughtiness and pride, which the girls gathered about them like protective shawls against the chill of modest circumstances. She found them singularly uneducated and said so, and surprised Lady Beverley by stating she would like to educate them all. So, having exacted a promise that they would learn "ladylike skills" as well, Lady Beverley gave her permission, and the mutinous Beverley sisters found themselves back in the schoolroom, a dingy room at the top of the house that they considered suitable quarters only for servants. They had to learn all those "masculine" sciences such as mathematics, physics, and chemistry. Hitherto their education had been confined to a little French and Italian, sewing, and playing the pianoforte. In vain did Jessica protest to her mother that gentlemen did not like educated ladies. Lady Beverley was too impressed by the breeding and grace of this new governess. Besides, her days were taken up sitting at the window of her drawing-room and looking across the fields in the direction of Mannerling, as if waiting for some angel to waft her to her "rightful" home.

Jessica and the others finally settled down under Miss Trumble's rule, for in their period of mourning there was little else to do, and after a time, much as they grumbled, they began to take their lessons seriously.

Miss Trumble was just beginning to hope, as the warm days of summer arrived, that her charges had begun to forget their ambitions.

And then, one beautiful summer's day, a footman from Mannerling arrived. It was Lizzie, looking down from the schoolroom window, who recognized his livery and let out a little shriek and then cried out, "A footman from Mannerling!"

"Sit down!" Miss Trumble snapped. But a flurry of disappearing muslin skirts as the sisters scampered inelegantly down the stairs was her only answer. She shut the book she had been reading. She gave a little sigh. She had hoped that by strengthening and improving their minds through education she could combat the obsession with Mannerling.

Downstairs, lessons and Miss Trumble were forgotten as all exclaimed over the precious invitation to a ball at Mannerling "in honour of the return of our son, Harry."

Mrs. Kennedy, Lord Fitzpatrick's aunt, had taught them all how to make over their old dresses, but now the thought of having nothing new to wear was nigh unbearable.

Nevertheless, Lady Beverley proved adamant. Much as she shared her daughters' obsession with Mannerling, she had also become obsessed with saving pennies. As she had been profligate in the past, now she had become almost miserly. "You still have beautiful ball gowns," she protested.

"Everyone has seen them," wailed Rachel. The others pleaded in various ways for new gowns. "No," said their mother firmly. "We must make do. It is more important to arrive in style. We cannot all fit into our own little carriage, and so a carriage must be hired and coachman's livery must be found for Barry."

Miss Trumble appeared among them. "You must return to your lessons, girls," she said.

"Such momentous news!" exclaimed Lady Beverley. "We are to go to a ball at Mannerling."

"When, my lady?" asked Miss Trumble.

"Why . . . next week, next Friday."

"And you will accept such an invitation?"

Lady Beverley looked at the governess in surprise. "Why not, you odd creature? Have we not all been waiting and praying for such an invitation?"

"All the invitations were issued three months ago, or so I learned at the market at Whitsun, all the *other* invitations. Surely to receive yours now is an insult."

"I do not look at it that way," said Lady Beverley mulishly. "Why, 'tis an oversight, that is all. Of course we shall go."

"As you will," said Miss Trumble quietly. "Come now, ladies, return to the schoolroom."

"But there is so much to do," said Jessica haughtily. "This is more important than poring over a lot of silly old books."

"I do think," put in Lady Beverley, "that my dear girls should be excused from lessons until after the ball is over."

"So be it," said Miss Trumble. "It goes against the grain, my lady, to be paid wages and not to earn my keep."

"Oh, that is true, very true," said Lady Beverley who had conveniently forgotten the governess's pay last quarter-day. "Off with you, my chucks. We will look over your gowns this evening."

Scowling and muttering rebelliously, the sisters went back up to the schoolroom.

In the evening, while the girls fretted over their ball gowns, Miss Trumble let herself out into the garden. The air was cool and sweet. The sun was going down behind the trees. She gave a little sigh. She felt defeated. There was so much good in "her" girls. The lateness of the invitations was insulting. They should not have accepted. "Evening, miss," said a voice behind her. She swung round. The stocky, reassuring figure of Barry Wort stood there in the evening light.

"Good evening, Barry." Miss Trumble had a sudden desire to talk to someone, anyone, anyone at all who was not obsessed with Mannerling.

"Walk with me a little," she ordered. "How goes the vegetable garden?"

"Very fine, miss," said Barry. "More than plenty for the table."

They walked around the side of the house and so into the herb-scented calm of the kitchen garden.

"There is great excitement in the house," said Miss Trumble. "Late invitations to the Mannerling ball, and yet they are going."

"Of course, miss. If I may be so bold, to my reckoning they would have accepted the invitations had they arrived on the day of the ball itself."

"Quite." Miss Trumble half turned away. She should not be gossiping about her "betters" with a lower servant. But she turned back and pulled her shawl more tightly about her thin shoulders. "I am . . . concerned for them. From what I hear, at least Miss Isabella did not seem to be possessed with the same demons."

"I am afraid that was not the case," said Barry. "I worshipped Miss Isabella–Lady Fitzpatrick, that is. But somehow she will always be Miss Isabella to me. Miss Isabella writes to me. Having been cured of all her longing for her old home, she is now concerned about her sisters. Did they tell you that Miss Lizzie tried to commit suicide?"

"Over Mannerling? Over a *house*?"

"Yes, miss. Tried to drown herself in the river. Lord Fitzpatrick, he rescued her."

Miss Trumble looked at him consideringly. Here was someone worth knowing. She could understand why the eldest Beverley sister wrote to him. He exuded a trustworthiness and calm that she found most endearing.

"What can we do to save them?" she heard herself asking.

Barry stooped down and pulled out a weed. Then he straightened up and looked at her seriously. "I have thought and thought, miss, and I have come to the conclusion that nothing but fate and God can do anything. I say my prayers for them nightly. I know more about these Deverses than even they do, servants being party to gossip between households. They are monstrous cold and proud and haughty, worse than the Beverleys ever were at the height of their glory. It is Miss Jessica who is setting her cap at Harry Devers. I have found, miss, that the only cure for false pride is humiliation. They will not receive the special treatment they still expect when they go to the ball. That might go a little way towards bringing them to their senses."

"And yet I would protect them from such a lesson," said Miss Trumble, half to herself.

Barry looked at her curiously. "I am a retired army man, miss, and have not been in service as an odd man for very long, but I have a sharp eye for quality. You do not seem at all like a governess to me."

Miss Trumble looked amused. "And what are governesses like, Barry?"

He scratched his head. "They're always reckoned to be poor things, miss. Neither fish nor fowl, bullied by their charges and treated badly by the lower servants. But to my mind, you seem more like the lady of the house at times than my Lady Beverley."

Miss Trumble smiled. "A great compliment, and I thank you."

"Mr. Ducket, Sir William's secretary, called on quarter-day to help my lady with the servants' wages, and the maid, Betty, did hear him ask as to why you had not been paid and my lady said, 'Perhaps later. Miss Trumble is on trial.' "

"Ah, as to that, I had no immediate need of money, having saved from my previous employ. But thank you for telling me this. I shall demand my wages immediately. There was no question of a trial, believe me."

Miss Trumble said good night to him and returned to the house. Bracing her shoulders, she went into the parlour where Lady Beverley was seated at her desk, going over the household accounts.

"My lady," began Miss Trumble.

Lady Beverley turned round and gave a gracious smile. In that moment, the ghost of a pretty young girl appeared momentarily behind her faded and discontented features, showing that she had once been as beautiful as her daughters.

"I did not receive my wages on quarter-day, my lady."

Lady Beverley stood up and began to walk about the room, picking things up and then discarding them. "As to that," she said finally, "I understood you were here on trial, and I have not yet received your references."

"I was not aware that I was here on trial. Perhaps I should seek other employ?"

"No, no," said Lady Beverley with a trace of petulance in her voice that showed she had realized she would have to pay the governess's wages after all. She was proud of this elderly governess with her aristocratic air and manners, which Lady Beverley felt added to the family's consequence. "I shall have the money for you in the morning. I would also like you to accompany us to this ball."

"In what capacity, my lady?"

"Why, as chaperone to my girls."

"But you will be there yourself, and I have not been invited."

"No matter," said Lady Beverley haughtily. "I will send a note by Barry informing the Deverses that you will be accompanying us."

Miss Trumble was about to protest, but the protest died on her lips. She was suddenly curious to see for the first time this great mansion that held the Beverleys in thrall.

Jessica peered round her bedroom door and watched the thin, erect back of the governess ascending to her room at the top of the house. She waited until the bobbing light of Miss Trumble's bed-candle had disappeared around a turn in the stairs before she retreated into her room and firmly closed the door.

"Now we can talk freely," she said to her sisters, who were sprawled about the room. "To be fair, one cannot expect such as a mere governess to understand our love of Mannerling. Do you think Mr. Harry Devers will be fetched by the blue muslin or the white?"

Rachel said, "I think you should borrow my silver overdress."

"But that is your favourite, besides being quite the prettiest thing you have."

Abigail, Rachel's twin, said, "But it is you, Jessica, who is to marry Mr. Devers and get our home back for us, so I think you should have the pick of what we have."

The others murmured their agreement.

Lizzie looked around at her sisters. "If only we knew more about these Deverses. Barry could tell us, I am sure, but Mama says we are not to speak to him or to any of the other servants."

"Quite right, too," said Belinda languidly. "We had begun to forget our station in life."

"And yet," said Abigail, her fair hair glinting in the soft light from the oil-lamp, "servants' gossip could be so useful. All we know is that the Deverses are very high in the instep."

"So are we," said Jessica. "It means they will not have vulgarized Mannerling like Mary and the dreadful Judd did."

"Try on your ball gown and let's have a rehearsal," urged Lizzie.

So, laughing and giggling, they helped Jessica into the white muslin gown and the silver gauze overdress. Abigail then acted the part of Harry Devers, and Jessica flirted so outrageously that they were soon all helpless with laughter.

Upstairs Miss Trumble heard that laughter and wished in her heart that all the joy and excitement were for a worthier reason.

Two days before the ball, Miss Trumble gave up all efforts at trying to teach her overexcited charges, and obtained Lady Beverley's permission to take the carriage into the neighbouring town of Hedgefield. Barry was driving. It was another perfect day. Miss Trumble realized as they drove farther away from Brookfield House that she had been beginning to find the atmosphere of almost mad excitement very disturbing. How five intelligent and beautiful girls could suddenly decide that it was only a matter of time before they all returned to Mannerling was beyond her. If by any remote chance Harry Devers proposed to Jessica and married her, what then? How could the rest of the Beverley family take up residence, with Mr. and Mrs. Devers very much alive? Besides, there had been no gossip at all about young Harry planning to sell out of the army. He was home only on leave.

"Is Mannerling so very beautiful?" she asked Barry.

"So people do reckon, miss," said Barry. "I can't see it myself, having taken the place in dislike on account of what it nearly did to Miss Isabella, not to mention poor little Miss Lizzie trying to drown herself."

"Is it haunted?"

"No, but twill be if there are any more deaths. John, an oily footman who worked for the Beverleys, then Mr. Judd and who is now with the Devers told me last market day that he had seen the ghost of Mr. Judd, but he always was a silly fellow."

"Have you see the Devers?" asked Miss Trumble as they began to drive into the centre of Hedgefield.

Barry nodded. "They were in town last market day. Why, there they are!" He pointed with his whip.

A tall lady and gentleman were standing outside the Green Man, followed by a lady's maid and two footmen. Mrs. Devers was expensively and fashionably gowned. Her husband was a miracle of good tailoring. He wore a white wig, curled and pomaded under a high-crowned beaver. With them was a younger man, possibly in his early thirties. He was standing with his hat in his hand. His black hair was cut in a fashionable Brutus crop. He had a clever, handsome face, a proud nose, and intelligent black eyes.

"That must be Mr. Harry with them," said Barry, "although he's older than I was led to believe."

For the first time, Miss Trumble began to have some hopes about the Devers. Mr. and Mrs. Devers were pretty much what she had imagined them to be. But their son appeared intelligent, good humoured, and very, very attractive.

Perhaps this ball might not be so bad after all.

Jessica found herself becoming increasingly nervous about the ball. It is very easy to allow other people to put you into roles and you may end up acting that role for the rest of your life. Jessica had certainly maintained that Isabella lacked "bottom," that she should have kept her sights on Mannerling and forgotten about love, the implication being that she, Jessica, would never have been so weak. And so her sisters looked up to her as a strong character, the sister of iron, and Jessica came to believe that was exactly what she was. But when she was alone, she felt weak and vulnerable and prey to doubts. Had her parents been more loving and less proud, then perhaps Manerling would not have been so predominant in her thoughts. As children when they long for home think of their mother and father, so Jessica thought of the cool elegant rooms of Mannerling and remembered her days there as being full of sunshine and laughter, which had not been at all the case. She forgot that her hitherto uneducated mind had made many of the days long and tedious, particularly after the long winters set in.

So basically rather timid and shy, Jessica, like most shy people, found it easier to play the part thrust on her and the bolder and "clear-headed" she seemed in her ambitions, the more her sisters appeared to admire her.

She was taking one of her solitary, restless walks around the garden one evening when she was joined by Lizzie. Like her sisters, Jessica never liked to dwell too deeply on Lizzie's attempted suicide, putting it down to the temporary madness of a delicate nature. As other girls might find excuses for the monstrous behaviour of a drunken father, so did Jessica shy away from the truth that an obsession with Mannerling had nearly killed Lizzie.

But Lizzie with her fey features seemed quite cheerful and relaxed as she smiled up at her sister, but then she, thought Jessica with another stab of worry, was not obliged to save the family fortunes.

"It is all very exciting, is it not?" ventured Lizzie. "Of course you will be successful, Jessica. You always are."

"At what?" asked Jessica with a sudden stab of cynicism. "I have been hitherto put to no great test apart from deciding which gown to wear."

"But you are so strong!" said Lizzie, her green eyes alight with admiration, that admiration which was so essential to the bolstering of Jessica's flagging spirits.

"Lizzie," protested Jessica, "you are surely the only one who will not be disappointed if I fail. As you said, it is only a building."

"That was before the invitations came," said Lizzie. "I could not help remembering how upset and miserable Isabella was when she thought she had to marry Mr. Judd. But you will not be like that, Jessica. Nothing worries you. I envy you."

"What worries me," said Jessica slowly, "is that if I fail, you might try to do something stupid again, Lizzie."

"No, no," said Lizzie quickly. "I am so ashamed of that. I would never try to take my own life again, no matter what happened. I . . . I love you, Jessica, and I am most proud of you."

Jessica's eyes filled suddenly with tears and she turned her head away, glad of the increasing darkness of the summer's evening. She wished suddenly for someone to lean on, someone in whom she could confide her weakness.

"Come in, girls. You are out in that damp night air, are

you not?" came Lady Beverley's voice from the parlour window.

Lizzie turned and scampered back towards the house. With lagging steps, Jessica followed her.

Chapter Two

Ha! ha! Family Pride, how do you like that, *my buck?*

—*W. S. Gilbert*

On the day of the ball, Brookfield House was filled with the smells of lotions, pomades, washes, and hot hair from the frequent use of curling tongs.

To the sisters' surprise, Miss Trumble insisted on helping with the preparations, and proved to be an excellent hairdresser. She also knew how to drape a shawl to perfection and how to make head-dresses of real flowers.

Jessica felt the day was flying past at a great rate. She had hoped it would go more slowly so that she could dream, could savour the moment when she would be back at Mannerling again.

But all too soon the great moment arrived when they climbed into the rented carriage with Barry up on the box in a second-hand livery and white wig and cocked hat. It was a tight squeeze inside the carriage, and the sisters squabbled about crushed gowns. But as they turned in at the great gates of Mannerling, an almost religious silence fell on them.

Miss Trumble found herself becoming nervous. In their silence, the Beverley sisters seemed fragile and vulnerable.

Then the carriage stopped. Miss Trumble followed them out and stood for a moment looking up at the house. It was large and graceful, with two wings springing out from a central block and a porticoed entrance, but she could not see that it was anything out of the common way.

In silence they entered the hall. It was imposing. A double staircase rose from the hall to the chain of saloons on the first floor where the ball was being held. White marble statues of Roman gods and goddesses stood on the white-and-black-tiled floor. Huge arrangements of hothouse flowers scented the air. They went to the room off the hall to leave their wraps; the housemaid Betty, elevated to lady's-maid, following them. It was when they were ready to go out again and up the stairs that Lady Beverley noticed with surprise the richness of her governess's gown. Miss Trumble was wearing a dull-gold silk gown of a cut that Lady Beverley felt was more modish than her own. "You are very fine, Miss Trumble," she said with a sour note in her voice. "My previous employer was very generous," said Miss Trumble placidly. "This is one of her gowns. Shall we go upstairs?"

Lady Beverley led the way and the others walked behind. Miss Trumble hoped that the Deverses would not protest at her presence. But when she curtsied to Mr. and Mrs. Devers and their son Harry, she promptly forgot her own worries in a sharp stab of disappointment. For Harry was not the attractive, intelligent-looking man she had seen outside the Green Man in Hedgefield. Certainly Harry Devers was handsome, tall with fair hair and fine grey eyes. He had a square jaw and trim waist. But there was a raffishness emanating from him, and she did not like the way his eyes ranged over the sisters, settling on Jessica with a predatory look.

They went on into the ballroom, which was composed of three saloons. Under the painted ceilings, dancers were performing the cotillion. "Dear me," said Jessica, fanning herself vigorously, "there is Mary Stoppard; I mean Mary Judd. Also, there are a number of quite undistinguished people here."

"Mannerling looks beautiful," said Lizzie. "Do you think they still have the portraits of our ancestors in the Long Gallery?"

"It does not matter," said Jessica. "Mr. Harry is an extremely handsome and agreeable man, do you not think?"

When the cotillion ended, Miss Trumble saw with satisfaction that all her charges had partners for the next dance, and so she made her way to a row of chairs against the wall. She sat down next to a stout lady who introduced herself as Miss Turlow. On learning she was sitting next to a mere governess, Miss Turlow was inclined to cut this Miss Trumble, but her desire for gossip was too great.

"I am surprised to see the Beverleys here," began Miss Turlow. "I heard from my maid that the Deverses finally decided to invite them because they thought it might be sport to watch one of the young ladies trying to ensnare their son. I called at the vicarage and I said to Mrs. Judd that they would not come, being insulted by such a last-minute invitation, but she said they would be so desperate to see if there might not be any way they could get their hands on Mannerling again, that no insult would stop them from attending."

Miss Trumble stood up, turned and looked down at Miss Turlow. "You are a malicious and unkind gossip," she said. She walked away and left an enemy behind her.

But try as she would, Miss Trumble could not quite escape hearing more cruel gossip about the Beverleys. Her heart sank. Their ambition was so obvious, so vulgarly obvious, and they had probably offended quite a number of people in the days of their greatness. She at last found a seat in a corner.

"May I fetch you some refreshment, ma'am?" The voice was husky, light, and pleasant. She looked up into the face of the man she had mistaken for Harry Devers.

"You are most kind. A glass of champagne would be most welcome."

He bowed and went off and then returned after only a few minutes carrying two glasses of champagne. He handed one to her, looked around, saw a small rout chair a little way away, fetched it, and drew it up next to her.

"You should be dancing with the pretty ladies," said Miss Trumble. "But thank you for the champagne. You are a relative of the Deverses?"

"I am Harry's cousin. Allow me to present myself. Robert Sommerville, at your service."

"I am Miss Trumble, governess to the Beverley sisters."

"Ah, the beautiful Beverleys. They used to live here, did they not?"

"Yes, Mannerling was once their home."

"We are in the same line of business, Miss Trumble."

"Indeed, sir? You look much too grand to be a tutor."

"And you appear too *grande-dame* to be a governess. I am a professor at Oxford University."

"Of what, sir?"

"Dead languages, Miss Trumble. Latin and Greek."

"Ah, that explains it."

"My dry-as-dust manner?"

"No, sir. I saw you in Hedgefield and thought you might be the son of the house. By your clothes and manner, you could be any Bond Street aristocrat, were it not for your obvious intelligence."

"And you do not credit dandies with intelligence?"

"I am often too severe in my judgements, I admit."

"You said you were governess to the Beverley sisters."

"I did."

"But not to all of them? The beauty of the family, the eldest, is surely past the age of needing a governess."

"I am unusual in that I consider a few ladylike accomplishments do not make an education. With Lady Beverley's permission, I am educating them in what I consider a proper manner, that is, in mathematics, physics, and chemistry. We have not yet started on the dead languages."

"You will turn them into the sort of ladies a man like me dreams about, beautiful *and* educated."

"You are a *rara avis,* sir. Most gentlemen are supposed to prefer stupid women." She gave a little sigh. "I have certainly found it so."

"If that is the case, and you have five marriageable young ladies to school, why did you decide to give them the sort of education usually only taught to men?"

"In the hope that they can produce intelligent sons, but more than that. When their looks have gone, they will need something to furnish their empty days."

His black eyes were shrewd and sympathetic. Did Miss Trumble feel she had once lost love through being too clever?

Lady Beverley appeared before them. Miss Trumble rose to her feet, as did Robert Sommerville. She introduced him. Lady Beverley, on learning that he was a relative of the family, was all that was gracious, but she was annoyed with her governess, who had no right to be sitting chatting with a guest on what had looked from across the floor to be equal terms. Besides, her gown was much too modish for her lowly station. "I would like you to find Betty and fetch my vinaigrette," said Lady Beverley.

Miss Trumble curtsied and left. "You are fortunate in having such a charming and highly intelligent governess," said Robert.

Lady Beverley promptly forgot that she had been annoyed with the governess. "You have the right of it. We Beverleys can still command the best."

Her face brightened perceptibly. Robert followed her gaze. Harry Devers was dancing with Jessica. They made a handsome couple. Jessica's silver overdress and filmy muslin gown floated out around her body. It was the year in which skirts had been raised enough to show a glimpse of the ankles. Jessica Beverley's were excellent, thought the professor dreamily. He decided to see if he could secure a dance with her, preferably the supper one, to see if her character matched her beauty. Then he smiled to himself. If Harry

Devers had not already secured that supper dance, then someone else must have booked it.

He realized Lady Beverley was fluting on about the great days of Mannerling—the great days when the Beverleys had been in residence—and suddenly bored and irritated, he waited until she paused to draw breath, rose and bowed and said he must go and talk to a friend. Miss Trumble returned with the vinaigrette. "Quite a pleasant fellow," remarked Lady Beverley.

"And a good catch," said Miss Trumble.

Lady Beverley gave a pitying laugh. "Any of my daughters can command better than that."

Harry Devers was bowing before Jessica. The dance had finished. Jessica looked radiant. Miss Trumble felt depressed and wished she could go home.

Jessica herself was confident that Harry Devers would invite her for the supper dance. She basked in the delight and admiration on her sisters' faces. But when the supper dance was announced, Harry Devers asked another young lady and Jessica stood with a bright smile pinned on her face, trying hard, Miss Trumble noticed gloomily, to look as if she cared not a whit. In fact, her other courtiers, since all knew of the Beverleys' ambitions, had also assumed that Harry would ask her for the supper dance, and for a few moments it looked as if Jessica, the belle of the ball, would have to join the wallflowers. But then Robert Sommerville approached her. Jessica was so relieved that she would not have to take supper with her mother and the other chaperones that she smiled bewitchingly at Robert and danced the waltz with him so gracefully that the normally hard-headed professor felt bewildered by a series of new emotions. He had rather hoped to find her empty-minded and silly so that he need not feel obliged to warn her against Harry. He knew that Mr. Devers had in the past had to buy Harry out of trouble, and one of those troubles, it had been whispered, had been the rape of an officer's wife. But Mrs. Devers had assured him that Harry was a reformed character. All he needed to complete his reformation was a suitable bride. So why not stand back and let Jessica Beverley achieve her ambition? They had not talked much on the dance floor. Perhaps, over supper, she would prove to be empty and vain.

But as Robert was leading Jessica to the supper-room, Jessica's sharp ears caught a remark made by Miss Turlow. She heard that lady's reedy voice murmuring, "So Mr. Harry has become wise to the ambitions of the Beverleys. So blatant. Of course, that vulgar governess of theirs must surely encourage them to make such obvious cakes of themselves."

Jessica felt herself beginning to blush deep-red. Robert Sommerville was saying something to her, but she could not hear the words because of a roaring in her ears. She had been told all her life about how elegant and superior the Beverleys were, how far above common mortals. To be exposed as a vulgar man-hunter was nigh past bearing. With a great effort, she recovered her composure. If her behaviour in pursuing Harry Devers was that obvious, then she must begin to look as if she had no interest in him at all. So when the professor asked her about her unusual education, she gave him her full attention, saying, "At first it was irksome. I did not want to return to the schoolroom, having escaped it. But then I began to enjoy it. The days pass so easily when one is occupied."

"I wish my students shared your enthusiasm," said Robert.

"You are a tutor?"

"I am a professor of Latin and Greek at Perry College, Oxford."

"I always thought professors would be very, very old and dull. How did you get a professorship so early in life?"

"I am thirty-five. You flatter me. Mr. Devers presented a handsome library to the college. You could say I had unfair influence."

"Did you feel you did not deserve the appointment?"

"In a world where all appointments are based on influence rather than merit, it did not trouble me overmuch."

"Is it not a boring life?"

"A cloistered life among the bachelors. I am unusual in that I have not taken holy orders."

"What if you should marry?"

"Ah, then I should retire happily to my home in the country."

"You have an estate?"

"I have a tidy mansion and five hundred acres in Gloucestershire."

"You cannot see much of it."

"On the contrary, I am at home quite a lot in term time and during the long recess. I have an excellent factor, so the estate is well run in my absence."

"Is your house like Mannerling?"

"No, it is not very grand, quite modest, built only in the last century. No ghosts, no long history."

"No ghosts?"

Robert gave his charming, husky laugh. "I do not believe in ghosts, Miss Beverley. Do you?"

"I do not know. Perhaps the last owner of Mannerling, Mr. Judd, who hanged himself, walks at night."

"I doubt it. I do not see Mrs. Devers putting up with a stray ghost in her home."

"You are a relative, I gather?"

"Yes, Mr. Devers is my uncle, my mother's brother. So Harry is my cousin."

Jessica tried hard not to look as interested as she felt. "What is Mr. Harry like?"

"Very wild, I believe."

"But he is an army man, and all army men are wild."

His black eyes mocked her. "You knowing so many army men?"

She gave a reluctant laugh. "But Mr. Harry is young, is he not? He will settle down."

"Some men never settle down. He is twenty-seven. Hardly a lad." He changed the subject abruptly. "Do you miss Mannerling?"

"So very much," said Jessica.

"But it is just a house."

"It is more than just a house to us. We were so happy here. We had many servants and every comfort and never thought things would change."

"As you can command a governess of the calibre of Miss Trumble, you can hardly be living in poverty."

"We are comfortable enough," said Jessica reluctantly. "But it is not the same."

"Perhaps the road to happiness lies in an acceptance of what one has got."

"How true and how tedious of you to point that out. If we all believed that, then what would happen to our dreams?"

"What indeed?" he countered, his eyes noticing the beauty of her shining auburn hair, the thickness of her lashes, and the purity of her skin. "I am talking too much and keeping you from this delicious food."

"Gunter's," she said wistfully. "Gunter's of Berkeley Square. They did the catering for us at the last ball we held at Mannerling. That was where Isabella, my elder sister, met her husband. And then, shortly after that, we learned Papa had lost everything."

"I heard of your father's death." His eyes took in the beauty of her fine muslin gown and silver overdress. "But you are not even in half mourning!"

"Life goes on," said Jessica sententiously. "Such mourning clothes as we had were rather inexpertly dyed black by ourselves, and creating half mourning would mean a tedious amount of work."

There was a dry note in his voice as he said, "You must miss your father."

She flushed slightly. The truth was that they all felt so bitter about Sir William's losing Mannerling that they had not mourned him very much. He had always been a remote, rather strange figure to Jessica. For the second time that evening, she felt ashamed of herself and out of charity with this professor, who talked to her with such familiar ease as if he had known her a long time instead of having only met her that evening.

His eyes teased her as she picked at her food. "I am a bear and a bad escort. I should be telling you how very beautiful you are and how fast you make my heart beat."

Jessica was about to give him a frosty glare, but in that moment she saw Harry Devers watching her and so she gave Robert Sommerville a languishing look instead, and said flirtatiously, "I do not believe you are a dry-as-dust professor at all. I think you are a ladies' man."

"Heaven forbid. That is Harry's role."

"Who is that lady with Mr. Harry?"

"That is a new addition to the county, Miss Habard. A very rich heiress and accounted a beauty until set against the Beverley sisters."

The reality of the fact that she herself must have little or no dowry to offer any prospective husband hit Jessica like a blow. This was an age of "business" marriages. Rank was important, but money was the most important thing of all. No matter how rich the family, they never encouraged their sons or daughters to marry anyone with less.

A great weariness stole over Jessica. She had been so elated earlier in the evening, basking in her sisters' admiration, confident that all their worries and humiliations were over. Now it all seemed hopeless.

Such was Jessica's obsession with Mannerling that she was not aware that she was taking supper with a rich and eligible man. Mannerling seemed to call to her, Mannerling seemed to mourn with her.

Then, for the first time, her own obsession appeared ridiculous to her. Her brain felt clear and light. She had been wasting her young life on a dream. All she had to do was to let go of it, forget Mannerling, forget Harry Devers, and then surely there was so much in her life she could enjoy.

Robert, who was sitting next to her, wondered what she was thinking. One moment her face had been dark and sad, and then her eyes were suddenly filled with light and relief, like someone waking from a nightmare.

She turned to him. "Poor Mr. Sommerville, I have not been very good company. I fear I have wasted a great deal of time mourning the loss of my old home. It is only bricks and mortar after all."

He felt light-hearted. He filled her glass with more wine. "A toast to the death of Mannerling," he said.

Jessica laughed and raised her glass. "Rest in peace."

From across the room, Harry Devers watched Jessica's beautiful face. He had been warned by his mother that Jessica's only interest in him would be to get back into her old home. But she appeared entirely taken up with Robert. Robert was a good-looking fellow, he thought sourly. Jealousy began to rise in him. He paid no attention to what his partner was saying and watched Jessica's every move, every expression.

As soon as the supper was over, Harry made his way to her side and requested the next dance. It was a country dance, so he did not have much opportunity to talk to her, but when they walked around the floor in the promenade at the end, he said, "I must ask your parents' permission to call on you. Would you find that agreeable, Miss Jessica?"

"I should feel honoured," said Jessica politely. She saw Robert Sommerville watching her and smiled at him. Harry saw that smile and added quickly, in a low voice, "You enchant me. You are the most beautiful lady I have ever seen."

All Jessica's obsession came flooding back. She looked at him somewhat dizzily. He bowed over her and she curtsied. Her next partner claimed her and how she performed the dance, which was the quadrille, she did not know, for she was filled with such triumph and elation, she felt like shouting out loud.

Miss Trumble, who had come to know Jessica very well, felt her heart sink. For a short glorious time during supper, she had felt that Jessica and the attractive professor might make a go of it, but she had noted the way Harry had murmured something to Jessica and she had then become excited, nervous, and elated. Miss Trumble tried to remind herself severely that her job was to educate the Beverley sisters, not to run their lives or choose husbands for them. But she had become fond of them despite their pride, despite all their plots to return to Mannerling.

Robert Sommerville, too, had noticed the change in Jessica. At first he silently cursed Harry and then he shrugged. Jessica did not have the necessary strength of character that he looked for in a woman. No woman of any character would look twice at Harry. Jessica's ambition to reclaim Mannerling was all too patent.

But how very charming she had been for that short time when her obsession had left her!

Back at Brookfield House after the ball, the sisters waited eagerly until Miss Trumble had retired for the night and then they gathered in Jessica's bedroom and looked at her hopefully.

"He said," began Jessica, savouring her triumph, "that he would call on me."

The others cheered and clapped. "Shh!" admonished Jessica. "Miss Trumble will hear us. There is more!"

"Tell us," urged Rachel.

"He said, 'You enchant me. You are the most beautiful lady I have ever seen.' "

More laughter and clapping. "You are wonderful, Jessica," said Abigail. "You will not let us down the way Isabella did."

"But will you be happy?" asked Lizzie suddenly.

Jessica looked at her in irritation. Why did Lizzie have to introduce such a *serious* note? She felt all-powerful. It was a game, that was all. They were enjoying the spirit of the chase.

But, oh, why did Lizzie have to say that?

She managed to laugh and gossip with her sisters for a short while longer but she felt very relieved when they finally took themselves off.

She could feel the role she had adopted of strong, confident, successful Jessica beginning to crumble and she wearily stared at her reflection in the mirror and remembered how free she had felt when her desire for her old home had lifted. But then she thought about Harry's words. Everything would work out very well. He was handsome and charming. It was a pity he was in the army, but surely he would sell out once they were married.

She was doing the right thing. She was doing what was expected of her.

So why did she feel so . . . *shabby*?

Chapter Three

Come in the evening, or come in the morning,
Come when you're looked for, or come without
warning.

—THOMAS OSBORNE DAVIS

To the sisters' dismay, Harry Devers did not call in person the following day but sent a servant with his compliments.

Two more days went by while they tried to concentrate on their lessons. Because the weather was fine, Miss Trumble had confined lessons to the morning and suggested they went out for walks in the afternoon. Jessica was beginning to feel very low. She had been so sure Harry would call. On the afternoon of the third day they were returning from one of their walks–which Miss Trumble had been trying to enliven with a botany lesson–when Lizzie suddenly exclaimed, "There is one of the carriages from Mannerling!"

"Don't run," admonished Miss Trumble, as they all would have started to rush forward. "It is very wrong to look so eager."

They approached the house chatting loudly about the beauty of the weather and the countryside.

Betty, the little maid, bobbed a curtsy as she opened the door to them, informing Miss Trumble that "my lady and the gentleman are in the garden."

The enterprising Barry had created a smooth lawn at the back of the house and had made rustic furniture and a table, which he had placed under the shade of an old cedar tree.

Jessica said to the others, "You go ahead. I must change and look my best."

She went quickly up to her room, calling on Betty to help her. She selected a pale-blue muslin gown with a wide blue silk sash. It had deep flounces at the hem. She noticed with dismay that it was getting a little worn under the arms. All their fine gowns made by a famous London dressmaker could not be expected to last forever. Mrs. Kennedy, Lord Fitzgerald's aunt, had taught them to make over their old gowns, often in a less fussy and more elegant style. But they had not worked on their dresses for a long time. Betty ran from room to room, collecting a matching blue silk parasol from the twins' room and blue kid gloves from Belinda's wardrobe.

After half an hour of frenzied preparation, Jessica made her way downstairs and out into the garden. As she approached the party under the cedar tree she stopped for a moment, hurriedly masking her disappointment. For it was not Harry Devers who sat there but Robert Sommerville.

Lady Beverley hailed her eldest daughter with relief. She felt her governess had been monopolizing the conversation. The fact was that Robert found Miss Trumble the easiest to talk to.

He rose to his feet when Jessica joined them. "Miss Jessica," he said, "unless you want to take tea, I would appreciate a tour of the rest of the gardens."

Jessica quickly agreed, for she wanted to find out where Harry Devers was and whether he intended to call.

When Jessica and Robert had moved away out of earshot, Lady Beverley said, "I do hope that young man is not going to take her mind off her purpose."

"What purpose is that, my lady?" asked Miss Trumble.

"Harry Devers is a better prospect."

"In my opinion, Mr. Robert Somerville has the finer character," said Miss Trumble.

"No one asked you for your opinion," snapped Lady Beverley. "I will decide who is suitable for my daughter and who is not."

Rachel, Abigail, Belinda, and Lizzie exchanged little smiles. Miss Trumble saw those smiles and fought down her irritation. They had begun to like her and respect her, she was aware of that, just as she was now aware that ambition to get Mannerling back had drawn them together against her.

"There is not very much in the way of a garden to see," Jessica was saying.

"On the contrary," said Robert, looking around at the beginnings of an orchard and the well-kept grass, "someone has been hard at work."

"That is Barry, our odd man, he does the gardening as well," said Jessica. "But you must admit, we can hardly compete with the gardens at Mannerling."

"And why should you want to try?" asked Robert.

"It is simply when one has been brought up in a certain style, then it is difficult to adjust to a lesser," said Jessica patiently.

"But you have been here for some time now. You have surely adjusted yourself to your circumstances."

"It is hard," said Jessica, looking into his dark eyes for sympathy and finding none.

The fact was that Robert was beginning to chide himself for wasting time with this beautiful girl who appeared to have nothing in her mind expect a bitter longing to regain her home. Her next question, put with badly affected casualness, did not surprise him.

"And how goes Mr. Devers?"

"Father or son?" he asked, although he knew very well which one she meant.

"Mr. Harry Devers."

"I do not know. I believe he was still asleep when I left."

"Oh," said Jessica in a little voice.

They had reached the herb garden, where Barry was diligently working. A light breeze blew across the herbs, scenting the air and ruffling Jessica's auburn hair.

"Good morning, Barry," said Jessica. "This is Mr. Sommerville from Mannerling, come to admire your work." She pulled a leaf from a plant and raised it to her nose. "This smells beautiful. What is it?"

"Orange thyme, miss."

"You have done miracles here," said Robert.

"Have you been here before, sir?" asked Barry.

"Yes, it was owned by a distant relative of mine, an elderly lady, a Miss Dalman. She cared for neither plants nor flowers. It was a wilderness compared to this."

He and Jessica moved away. "That is a fine fellow," said Robert.

Jessica gave a little shrug. "I do not particularly notice servants." The minute the words were out, she regretted them.

He said in a stiff voice. "I must return. Make my goodbyes to your family. Your servant, Miss Jessica."

He bowed and strode away. Jessica felt a pang of regret, but she quickly dismissed it. Robert Sommerville was very well in his way, but Harry Devers was the quarry.

She returned to her sisters and mother. Lady Beverley looked up in surprise. "Where is Mr. Sommerville?"

"He has left, Mama."

"Without saying goodbye! How very odd. I am sure young Mr. Devers would not have behaved so."

"We are never likely to find out," snapped Jessica. She felt tetchy and ashamed of herself about the remark she had made about servants to Robert Sommerville. "I was mistaken in Harry Devers's interest in me, that is all."

Harry Devers was not thinking of anything much other than his aching head and dry mouth when he walked through to the Green Saloon at three in the afternoon that day. Robert Sommerville was sitting reading a newspaper. He put it down when Harry entered and said, "You look uncommon rough."

"Stayed awake till dawn finishing the brandy," said Harry, stifling a yawn.

"I have been about this age," said Robert, putting down the newspaper. "I called on the Beverleys."

"A beautiful nosegay of beauty," said Harry. "Oh, my curst head!"

He slumped down in a chair and looked vaguely about him. "I'm thinking of selling out."

Robert looked at him in surprise. "Leave the army! But you love the army."

"Fact is," said Harry, "I feel at home for the first time. I mean, here at Mannerling."

"I cannot understand the fascination of this place," remarked Robert. "It is a house, nothing more. Perhaps you should have called on the Beverleys." The latter was said sarcastically. Never for a moment did he think Harry would take him seriously.

Harry glanced at the clock. "I might just do that. There's still time. That Jessica is a prime piece of flesh and blood."

Robert stood up and loomed over Harry, suddenly a formidable figure. "Do you know something, Harry? I despise you and have always done so. Keep away from the Beverleys or I will be forced to tell Miss Jessica about your reputation."

Harry stared after him. Then he turned back and scowled at the wall. What reputation? He fancied himself as being irresistible to the ladies. Then his face cleared. Of course! That was it! Robert fancied the Jessica chit himself. He had taken her in to supper at the ball.

Harry got to his feet and went upstairs to his bedchamber, roaring for his valet and then shouting for his carriage to be brought to the front door. At last, barbered and changed into morning dress of blue swallow-tail coat, starched cravat, waistcoat embroidered with humming-birds, canary-coloured pantaloons, and glossy Hessian boots with little gold tassels, he made his way downstairs and out to his curricle.

As he approached Brookfield House, he noticed with satisfaction that it was quite a shabby place compared to Mannerling. But, then, nothing could rival Mannerling.

The sisters were in the garden. Lessons had been suspended for the day, but Miss Trumble was just beginning to think that had been a bad idea, for Jessica looked gloomy and disappointed and the rest were sitting idly under the cedar tree, also in the doldrums.

And then Betty, the little maid, came running into the garden, the streamers on her white cap flying. "Mr. Devers is here," she cried. "Mr. Harry Devers."

"Then show Mr. Devers into the garden," said Miss Trumble, "and tell your mistress he is come." She noticed that Jessica was now flushed and radiant and that her sisters were exchanging triumphant little looks. When Harry Devers sauntered into the garden, swinging his cane, walking with his feet pointed out to each side in that silly way gentlemen affected these days, Miss Trumble thought he looked more like a coxcomb than she had remembered him to be, but it was obvious that the Beverley girls saw no fault in him. Miss Trumble resolved that in this case, Jessica would stay where she was: no intimate walks in the garden with Mr. Devers.

"A charming sight on a beautiful day," said Harry, sweeping off his high-crowned hat and giving a low bow as the sisters and Miss Trumble dropped curtsies. How they fussed around him, offering him the most comfortable chair, putting a cushion at his back, asking if he would like any refreshment. Harry smiled languidly all about and said he would like a glass of wine, and Betty was sent running to fetch it. Miss Trumble was relieved to see Lady Beverley walking across the grass to join them, but her relief was short-lived, for after the pleasantries were over and Harry had drunk his glass of wine, Lady Beverley said, "Jessica, my dear, why do you not show Mr. Harry the garden?"

"I will accompany you," said Miss Trumble, rising to her

feet, but Lady Beverley said sharply, "Sit down, Miss Trumble. There are matters I wish to discuss with you."

So, for the second time that day, Jessica led a gentleman around the garden.

"The roses are beautiful, are they not?" Jessica bent down to smell one.

"Nothing in the world is as beautiful as you," said Harry. He briefly forgot about Jessica as he mentally paused to admire the stunning neatness of his compliment.

"You are too kind," murmured Jessica.

"Not kind. *Honest,* Miss Jessica."

Her bosom was soft and round. He fumbled for his quizzing-glass to get a better look at it and then decided such an action might be too bold.

"When do you return to the army?" asked Jessica, anxious to know how much time she had to make a conquest.

"As to that," he said, "I have been considering selling out."

"Is this a sudden decision?"

"In a way. I feel I have found a home at last."

"Ah, Mannerling," said Jessica wistfully.

"Yes. I never considered I was a sentimental sort of cove, and yet, there is something about the place . . ."

"It is the beauty of the design, the painted ceilings, the staircase, the formal gardens . . ."

"Miss it, do you?"

"Oh, so very much."

"Well, you must come over and see us and it. I'll tell Mama to expect you for tea tomorrow at three, say?"

"I would like that above all things. May I bring my family?"

"Maybe another time." Her mouth was beautifully shaped and pink. If he got her on her own at Mannerling, he could maybe steal a kiss . . . or more! "Come on your own."

"Very well," said Jessica.

"I'll say goodbye, then." He made a low bow and then

seized her hand and pressed it to his lips. He thought she blushed adorably. He left feeling pleased with himself. He found her very attractive. He had been warned of the Beverleys' ambitions, but there was no way he could have a girl like Jessica outside marriage. Besides, her enthusiasm for Mannerling matched his own. If he married her, then perhaps he could persuade his parents to live elsewhere and then have Mannerling all to himself.

Miss Trumble thought that here was another gentleman who had rudely left without saying goodbye to the rest of the family. But Jessica was all smiles as she told her rapt audience of her invitation to tea.

The worried governess decided to have a quiet word with her when she could get her alone, but that opportunity did not arrive until late in the evening when she saw Jessica go out into the garden and followed her.

A greenish sky pricked by the first star of evening stretched over the quiet garden. The air was warm and still.

"I wish to speak to you in private before you go to Mannerling tomorrow," said Miss Trumble.

"What about?" asked Jessica lazily. She and her sisters had discussed Jessica's "triumph" over and over again.

"I have met gentlemen like Mr. Harry Devers before," said Miss Trumble quietly. "They have strong, almost animal, appetites in their approach to women. To put it bluntly, you are an inexperienced virgin."

"And you, not being one, know so much better?" Jessica's fine eyes flashed in the twilight.

"Don't be impertinent or hoity-toity with me, miss. Your obsession with Mannerling is blinding you to Mr. Devers's faults. He dresses and acts like a coxcomb."

"I am not going to listen to any more of this," said Jessica furiously. "You forget your position in this household, Miss Trumble."

Miss Trumble looked at her haughtily. "I am never likely to be allowed to forget, am I? Very well, do what you must.

But do not come running to me for help."

"You? I would not dream of it."

"Let us not quarrel," said the governess in a calmer tone. "Mr. Sommerville, on the other hand, is all that a gentleman should be, and more."

The spoilt child which was still part of Jessica's character rose to the surface. "Why don't you marry him yourself?" she jeered, and then she turned on her heel and marched off to the house.

Miss Trumble sighed and sat down on a fallen log at the edge of the lawn.

"I must behave more like a governess," she said aloud.

"Is that difficult for you, miss?" said a voice behind her, making her jump.

She looked round and saw Barry standing there in the gloom. "You startled me," said Miss Trumble.

"I'm sorry, miss. I couldn't help hearing what you said, the garden being so quiet-like."

"I was talking to myself," said Miss Trumble. "A bad habit of old age. I merely meant that it is difficult to remember one's place when one is concerned with the folly of one's charges."

"They do seem mighty determined to get back to Mannerling, no matter what." Barry sat down beside her on the log.

"We have talked about this before. I fear for Jessica. There is something about Harry Devers I cannot like."

"I was with the other coachmen and servants at the ball, miss, and the gossip was that the ladies were not safe around him, and in this wicked day and age a gentleman has to be pretty bad for a bunch of male servants to think him shocking. But to put your fears at rest, Miss Jessica is determined to pursue him. But she will not be left alone with him."

"She was this afternoon, and with her mother's encouragement, too."

"Ah, yes, but that was in this garden, with me about and

the maids bound to be watching from the windows. What I am trying to say is that Mr. Harry will have little opportunity to molest Miss Jessica were he so inclined."

"And yet," said Miss Trumble bitterly, "I could find it in my heart to wish that he would give her a really good fright to knock some of the nonsense out of her head."

But Miss Trumble and Barry Wort were alone in their concern as next day Jessica set out for Mannerling accompanied by the maid Betty, and with Barry driving the small Beverley carriage. Her sisters and mother were there on the step to wave her goodbye.

Jessica felt happy and elated, and the only cloud on her horizon was the niggling memory of the contempt Robert Sommerville had shown her. She shook him off mentally. He did not matter. He was only a guest, after all.

The whole ambience of Mannerling seemed to enclose her in welcoming arms as the horse pulling the carriage clip-clopped sedately up the long drive. She let down the glass and gazed hungrily at the house, at the white pillars of the entrance, at the graceful wings on either side of the main building, and then across the grounds, across the smooth green of the lawns to the ornamental lake where ducks bobbed like toys on the glassy water.

The entrance hall smelt of pot-pourri and beeswax. She placed a loving hand on the shining mahogany of the banister, caressing its smoothness as if stroking the hand of the lover she had never known.

The butler ushered her into the drawing-room and announced her. Harry was there with his mother. There was no sign of either Mr. Devers or Robert Sommerville. Jessica was disappointed that Robert was not there. She knew she was looking her very best in a white lace morning gown with little puffed sleeves and a low neckline, and she wanted to show him that she did not care what he thought about her in the slightest. She gave Mrs. Devers her best court curtsy.

Mrs. Devers, small and elegantly gowned, returned the curtsy with a brief nod. Harry jumped to his feet and bowed.

Jessica sat between Mrs. Devers and Harry on a Chippendale chair, a Beverley chair, starting a little when a footman leaped to slide it under her bottom, something that, in the not-so-long past, she would have taken for granted.

Mrs. Devers made the tea herself, filling the delicate china pot from a silver urn over a little spirit stove.

Jessica took a cress sandwich and said, "The weather is holding fine."

Harry did not reply, for his mouth was full of cake. Mrs. Devers said nothing at all.

"The roses must make a fine display," pursued Jessica.

Mrs. Devers sipped tea, Harry ate another cake, the clock in the corner chimed a silvery three strokes, as if to remind Jessica that she had arrived a whole five minutes too early, and then silence settled on the room.

Jessica ate her sandwich. Mrs. Devers nodded to one of the two liveried footmen in attendance. One walked forward, picked up a plate of cakes, and offered it to Jessica. Jessica declined. She was determined now that Mrs. Devers should speak to her.

"You have added some charming touches," said Jessica, noticing the French clock, the Chinese wallpaper, and the new pianoforte.

"Aren't you going to eat anything else?" asked Harry, wiping his mouth with the back of his hand.

"No, I thank you." Jessica looked at Mrs. Devers as she spoke, but Mrs. Devers was slowly eating a slice of seed-cake, nibble, nibble, nibble, and continued to go on as if Jessica did not exist.

"In that case," said Harry, "I would like to show you the roses."

Jessica got to her feet. "I should like that. Pray excuse me, Mrs. Devers."

Mrs. Devers poured herself another cup of tea. Her cheeks

pink, Jessica allowed Harry to lead her from the room.

She could not help remembering when Mary, daughter of the vicar, had come to Mannerling to call in the old days. She and her sisters despised Mary as a toad-eater, and so they had decided one day to pretend she was invisible. How they had laughed about it afterwards. Jessica felt ashamed of herself now. She tried to remind herself that Mary was a creeping, slimy creature, and of how dreadful Mary had been when she had got her revenge on all of them by becoming, however briefly, mistress of Mannerling. But the shame she now felt would not go away. She said to Harry as he led her out of doors, "Your mother does not seem to relish my company."

"Hey, what's that? Mama? Oh, she has always been a trifle high in the instep, don't you know?"

"Do you mean she considers a *Beverley* beneath her?"

"I suppose she does. The rose garden is this way."

"I know," said Jessica crossly. "Why?"

"Why, what?" Harry was beginning to find Jessica a trifle fatiguing. Women were not for talking to, only for more interesting pleasures.

"Why on earth should Mrs. Devers consider me socially beneath her?"

"It's the talk of the neighbourhood how you lot would do anything to get your hands on Mannerling again."

The mortified pink on Jessica's cheeks deepened to a painful red. She had never stooped to consider for a moment that their ambitions should appear so transparent to Harry, despite what she had overheard at the ball.

"That is not true," she said furiously.

"Let's not jaw on about Mama. Ain't the roses fine?"

They had entered the rose garden, and were enclosed by roses and their heavy scent.

Harry decided it was time he made a move. He stopped and turned to face her. "I can understand your desire to get

Mannerling back," he said. "Damme, I love the place myself."

He suddenly seized her in his arms and kissed her hard.

Jessica did not experience any of the swooning rapture she had read about in novels. He had not been barbered properly and his chin felt scratchy and he smelt of brandy.

She disengaged herself as quickly as possible and said on what she hoped was a passionate sigh, "Why, Mr. Devers, you quite overset me."

"Thought I might," grinned Harry. He was about to try out a more intimate kiss when a footman came running up. "I beg your pardon, sir," he said, "but Mrs. Devers wishes you to return."

"Oh, blast it," said Harry wrathfully. "Can't a fellow get any peace?" He began to walk rapidly back to the house. Jessica ran for a little to try to keep up with him, but then slowed down and let him go ahead. She was suddenly revolted at her own behaviour, that she should put up with first being insulted by Mrs. Devers and then by Harry, who had not turned once to see whether she was following.

Now it seemed to her that Mannerling was a malignant presence sucking dignity and sanity from her. She quickened her step and went as far as the hall where the maid, Betty, was waiting patiently.

"We are leaving," said Jessica. She then summoned a hovering footman. "Be so good as to fetch my carriage, and tell Mrs. Devers I must go," she commanded haughtily.

And yet, as she waited outside with Betty for Barry to arrive, she began to feel a longing that Mrs. Devers would descend the stairs and come to ask her what the matter was, beg her to come back. But Barry arrived and jumped down to assist her into the carriage, his round honest face for once impassive. Jessica leaned back and fanned herself vigorously. She would face her sisters and tell them how she had been treated . . . and yet . . . and yet . . . he had kissed her. A gentleman did not kiss a lady unless his intentions were honourable and serious. How silly she had been to run away! She had an impulse to call to Barry to turn back but suppressed it. She had sent that footman with that message.

On her return she was aware of Miss Trumble's sharp scrutiny and did not want to describe her visit in front of the governess. She escaped with her sisters as soon as possible and they all walked to the far end of the garden.

"Well?" demanded Lizzie, her green eyes shining.

"It was difficult," said Jessica slowly. She began to describe Mrs. Devers's coldness, but when she got to the bit about Harry kissing her, they all laughed and clapped their hands.

"Capital!" cried Abigail. "He must propose marriage now!"

"But what if his mother and father won't let him?" asked Lizzie.

"Tish, he is a grown man and can do as he pleases," said Jessica airily, trying to show more confidence than she felt.

She might have been reassured could she have heard the conversation taking place at that moment in the drawing-room of Mannerling. Present were Harry, his father and mother, and Robert Sommerville.

"I have just been remonstrating with Harry," said Mrs. Devers. "I went to the window overlooking the rose garden and I saw him *kissing* that Jessica Beverley person. Then the Jessica person left, sending me a curt message of goodbye by my own footman."

"What did you expect?" demanded Harry. "You insulted her by pretending she did not exist. Course I told her you thought she was beneath you . . ."

"I am not surprised she left," said Robert drily.

Mr. Devers twisted his head so that he could see his son over the barrier of his high starched shirt-points. "You've made a bad mistake there, Harry, my boy. You'll have Lady

Beverley here on the doorstep demanding you marry the girl."

"And what would be so wrong with that?" demanded Harry. "You're always on at me to settle down."

"You cannot marry Jessica Beverley, and that is that," said his mother.

"No?" Harry rose to his feet and picked up a Dresden shepherdess from the mantel. "Like this piece, don't you, Mama?"

"Harry . . . don't," cried his mother, knowing her son's temper of old when he was thwarted.

Harry smiled at her, dropped the piece of fragile china on the carpet, stamped on it, and then ground the shards into the carpet with his boot. He walked to the door, saying over his shoulder, "I mean to have her, and marriage is the only way."

Robert Sommerville also rose to his feet. He saw in his mind's eye Jessica, beautiful and fragile like the piece of china which Harry had just broken. She must be made to see sense, made to see that her ambition to get Mannerling back was going to lead her to a life of shame and degradation.

Chapter Four

Marriage is like a cage: one sees the birds outside desperate to get in, and those inside equally desperate to get out.

—MICHEL DE MONTAIGNE

Early that evening, Lady Beverley was startled to receive the intelligence that Mr. Robert Sommerville had called again.

But she had finally heard Jessica's story of her visit to Mannerling and found nothing to be elated about, although she had kept her own council. For one moment, she felt it her duty to warn Jessica that contrary to popular opinion, a kiss did not mean a marriage. She considered Mrs. Devers's treatment of her daughter disgraceful, not recognizing in such haughty behaviour much of her own.

And so she graciously welcomed Robert, seeing in him some sort of thread that joined the Beverleys to Mannerling. Robert made general conversation and then said, seemingly idly, that as the evening was warm, he would be grateful if Miss Jessica could find the time to show him the garden again, as he had had to rush off the day before.

Jessica tried to signal with her eyes that she did not want to, but Lady Beverley said, "By all means."

"I thought you had seen enough of our gardens . . . and of me," said Jessica when they were clear of the house.

"I came to see you only because I thought it necessary. Harry Devers is determined to marry you."

He looked sadly at the glowing look Jessica gave him.

"There is nothing to be happy about, nothing to celebrate. I beg you to realize that the man is a brutal lecher."

Jessica was too happy and too elated to be angry. She thought he was jealous.

"I am persuaded you are too hard on him, sir," she said, wishing he would go and leave her to tell her family the marvellous news.

"No, I am not. He is also a drunkard and a wastrel. You think you would be happy to get Mannerling back again. But at what a cost! My dear, I am not jealous–I see you think I am–it is only that I cannot bear to see you ruined, and believe me, you would be ruined by such a marriage."

"I will not listen to you," said Jessica firmly. "You said you wished to see more of the gardens, so here we are in the gardens, sir."

"I have tried to do my duty," he said, half to himself. "I can do no more."

He looked around. They were screened from the house by a tall yew hedge. Jessica's face was alight with happiness in the setting sun. Despite her awful ambition, he sensed a sweetness in her. She had been warped by her upbringing, but her character could still be saved.

Before he could stop himself, he drew her into his arms. Jessica was too startled and surprised to resist. He bent his head and kissed her gently but firmly, full on the mouth. For one little moment, Jessica felt a surge of sweetness, of yearning, and then she pulled away and said breathlessly, "I think perhaps it is you and not Mr. Harry who is the lecher."

"That was a kiss from a man who respects you," he said, his black eyes fathomless. "The kiss you received from Harry in the rose garden was something else."

He turned and strode away. She watched him go, her hand to her lips, thinking how tall and athletic his figure was, thinking that he looked so little like a professor. Now she was free to tell her sisters of her success, but the elation she had felt when Robert had told her that Harry wanted to marry her was gone. She tried to tell herself that Robert's behaviour had been disgraceful, shocking. But the better side of her nature forced her to admit that he had been genuinely concerned about her, a concern that was entirely unnecessary, however.

Although the congratulations of her family raised her spirits, she was aware at the same time of Miss Trumble's eyes watching her with a look of pity.

After the next two weeks, the Beverleys, prepared every day for the arrival of Harry and his expected proposal, began to lose heart. Every day Barry had been sent over to the squire's with a request for ice to chill the champagne that was to be opened to celebrate the betrothal, until the squire rebelled and said his ice-house was becoming sadly depleted and the Beverleys could have no more.

And then the fine weather broke, not in a dramatic way either, but with a thin grey drizzle and mist. Jessica fretted. She thought and thought about the problem. She began to hate Robert Sommerville. He must have turned Harry against her. That must be it. Or could it be . . . could it be that they had got together and found that she had allowed *both* of them to kiss her? Although they had been stolen kisses, she had not, in either case, blushed or pushed either gentleman away. Day after grey day, she had to cope with her sisters' patent disappointment and her mother's voluble fretting about what had gone wrong.

One day, another rainy day, Jessica pleaded a headache in order to escape from the schoolroom. Miss Trumble let her go reluctantly. She did not believe Jessica had a headache but could think of no good reason to detain her.

Despite her mother's orders not to speak to the servants, Jessica was suddenly determined to seek out Barry and find out what was going on over at Mannerling. At the same time, she dreaded hearing that Harry had left to rejoin his regiment.

She slipped quietly into her bedroom and put a calash over her hair, pattens over her thin shoes, and a cloak around her shoulders, and then went out into the garden. At first she could not find Barry but then she heard sounds of activity coming from the garden shed. She pushed open the door and went in. Barry was sitting on a box in the corner, sharpening a scythe. He stood up when he saw Jessica.

"Good day," said Jessica awkwardly.

"May I be of service to you, miss?"

"I . . . I have never been in here before," said Jessica, looking around vaguely in the darkness of the shed at various implements and flowerpots. "How interesting."

Barry merely continued to look inquiringly at her.

Jessica drew forward another box and sat down with a little sigh. "You may continue your work, Barry."

Barry sat down obediently, picked up the stone, and recommenced sharpening the scythe with long, easy strokes.

"I wonder how they are getting on at Mannerling," said Jessica after some moments had passed. "Do you know if they are still in residence, Barry?"

He put down the stone and propped the scythe against the wall. "Yes, so I hear, Miss Jessica."

"So Mr. Harry has not yet rejoined his regiment?"

"No, miss. They had a big party for him the other day. Some of his army friends had come over. They had planned to have a fête in the gardens, but because of the bad weather it had to be held in the house."

"How odd that we were not invited," said Jessica. "But surely an oversight. Are you sure of this?"

"Yes, the vicar was talking about it the other day. He and his daughter, Mrs. Judd, were among the guests."

Jessica coloured with mortification. "Mrs. Devers cannot be as high in the instep as she pretends to be if that sorry couple were invited."

"As you know, Mrs. Judd does have encroaching ways."

I should not be talking like this with a servant, thought Jessica, but I must know more.

She tried to introduce a light, indifferent note into her voice as she asked, "Is Mr. Harry being pursued by all the ladies of the county?"

Barry did not want to tell her, but surely Miss Trumble, say, would point out that it was only for the girl's good. She had to know sometime.

"I think they have all given up hope," he said, not looking at her.

"And why is that?"

"They do say he has set his cap at Miss Habard."

"The heiress," said Jessica, half to herself. "The rich Miss Habard."

"The same."

Jessica tried to rally. "How people will gossip. It is probably a mere flirtation."

"Report has it that they are much taken with each other."

"Report, report," jeered Jessica. "The vicar's daughter again?"

"No, miss, it was Mrs. Devers herself."

"Now I know you are bamming me! Mrs. Devers talk to *you*!"

"No, of course not. I overheard her in the town, in Hedgefield. She was with that Mr. Sommerville, and she was telling him loudly about it and saying for all to hear that it was a suitable match."

"It is cold here," said Jessica with a little shiver. "Good day to you, Barry."

He watched her go sadly and then picked up the stone again and began to sharpen the blade of the scythe again, this time with savage strokes.

Miss Trumble looked up in surprise when Jessica reentered the schoolroom. "Why, Jessica," she said, "you do look rather pale. I thought you would lie down until your headache passed."

"I think I will feel better if I resume my studies," said Jessica, avoiding the scrutiny of her sisters. She wanted to bury herself in learning and never, ever think of Mannerling again.

But when the lessons were over, there was no escape. Her sisters followed her into the room. "What has gone wrong?" demanded Belinda. "Where did you go? I am sure you did not have the headache."

Jessica slumped down in an armchair and stared bleakly at the rain running down the window.

"I went to talk to Barry," she said.

"We have been told not to gossip to the servants," said Lizzie primly.

"How else was I to find out why he had not called?" asked Jessica.

"So what did he say?" demanded Abigail.

Jessica told them in a flat voice of what she had learned. "You see what this means?" she demanded. "We have no dowries to speak of. We are not even considered good enough to be invited to Mannerling any more, while such as Mary Judd is. I am sorry I have failed you, but there is nothing I can do. Mannerling is lost to us."

Miss Trumble reflected that surely no governess had ever had such dutiful charges. In the days succeeding Barry's bad news, the sisters, who had moved on to studying Latin and Greek, applied themselves so diligently to their work that Miss Trumble began to worry about them. When the weather turned fine again, she applied for permission from Lady Beverley to take them for walks and picnics. Lady Beverley gave that permission. She spent most of her days on a chaise longue in the parlour, doing nothing at all. Jessica's failure, of which she had been told, had seemed to make her mother lose interest in life itself.

Gradually fresh air and exercise and a desire to forget all about Mannerling improved the sisters' spirits. They became easier and friendlier. They even began to romp around with Lizzie, playing endless games of battledore and shuttlecock.

And that is how Robert Sommerville found them. He had gone back to his own home after his last confrontation with Jessica. But somehow he felt himself being drawn back to Mannerling. He had expected to see her with her family at the fête, but when he asked Mrs. Devers about the absence of the Beverleys, she had said haughtily that as Harry would shortly be betrothed to Miss Habard, she did not want any penniless beauty such as Jessica Beverley spoiling things.

In the hope that this latest snub had brought Jessica to her senses, he had ridden over. He dismounted and stood for a few moments watching the happy scene on the lawn. Jessica, animated and flushed and with her auburn hair tousled, was laughing as she darted here and there after the flying shuttlecock.

Miss Trumble was the first to see him. She thought again with a pang that he looked so strong and handsome compared to the feckless Harry. He was wearing breeches and top-boots and Miss Trumble gave a sentimental little sigh. His legs were excellent. The girls saw him. Jessica put her hand up to her tumbled hair and then took it away again, her face hardening. Had it been Harry, she would have rushed into the house to arrange her hair and change out of the old gown she was wearing. But Robert did not deserve such trouble.

Miss Trumble advanced, smiling a welcome. "How good to see you, Mr. Sommerville. Lady Beverley is resting."

The girls all curtsied, cold looks on their faces. They had all heard Jessica's speculation that Robert had turned Harry against her.

But when they were all gathered round the table under the cedar tree, the very fact that they had given up hopes of Mannerling made them realize that Robert was a charming man. He talked easily of his own home and the improvements he planned to make and then he asked if Jessica would walk with him for a little. Miss Trumble gave her permission and Jessica rose and went with him, wishing now she were wearing something prettier.

"I wished to speak to you in private," he said. "My behaviour when I last saw you was not that of a gentleman. Pray accept my humble apology."

Jessica nodded. "You are forgiven. We were both overset, I think."

He said awkwardly, "I am afraid that Harry is shortly to be betrothed to Miss Habard."

She gave a little sigh. "Fortune is so important in this day and age, is it not?"

"It is, and particularly among the richest families. I suppose that is why families like the Deverses are so rich. They always marry well. It can bring a great deal of sadness, young girls married to old men, or married to brutal husbands. Are you very disappointed?"

"No, it brought me to my senses. You must have noticed how happy we are now that we have no hopes of Mannerling. I shall never think of Mannerling again."

And in such a way, thought Robert sadly, he had heard hardened gamblers vow, "I will never play cards again," only to find them back at the tables the following week. He sent up a little prayer that Harry *would* marry Miss Habard, and as soon as possible.

Harry was at that moment leading Miss Habard towards the rose garden. She was not Jessica Beverley, he reflected, but a shapely little thing for all that, and with a roguish twinkle in her eyes that he liked. She had a profusion of glossy brown curls under a chip-straw bonnet and wore a thin muslin gown, which showed a great deal of her plump figure. The amount of white brandy he had consumed during the day was swimming pleasurably around his senses. He had brought Miss Habard to the rose garden to propose. He had called earlier that day on her parents and gained their permission. He knew they were abovestairs in the drawing-room with *his* parents, eagerly awaiting the happy announcement.

It seemed ages since he had had a woman, however, and his eyes gleamed with a feral look as Miss Habard dimpled up at him.

"You are a little charmer," he said. "Did I ever tell you that?"

"Oh, sir," said Miss Habard, blushing adorably, or so he thought.

Time to go into action. Get the proposal over with and then sample the wares.

He felt he should get down on one knee, but the fresh air was making him feel more tipsy and he didn't want to find out that he could not get up again. So he turned to face her and said huskily, "Do you know why I have brought you out here?"

Again that blush. She whispered, "Papa told me that you wish to marry me."

"Yes, my sweet."

"Oh, Mr. Devers, you make me the happiest of women."

"Thought I might," said Harry. "Yes, and I've decided to sell out."

"Papa told me you had said so, and he has chosen a tidy property for us quite nearby. It is the most darling house . . ."

"Wait a bit," said Harry angrily. "I will decide where we live, and we'll live here."

Miss Habard's slightly protuberant brown eyes looked up into his own with a stubborn expression. "Live at Mannerling, with your parents? It would not answer."

"I'll ask 'em to move out."

Her lip trembled. She took his arm and said coaxingly, "But you don't want to live in a great big place like this, do you?"

Her soft breast pressed against his arm. He could feel the heat from her body.

He said thickly, "Forget the house. We've got more enjoyable things to do."

He seized her in his arms and his mouth bore down on hers. His hands groped over delicious mounds of plump body, breasts, buttocks, and waist. His senses reeled and the rose garden swam away in a red mist and then through that mist he heard her crying and pleading, felt her hands hammering at his shoulders. A window above opened and his mother's voice shouted out, sharp with alarm, "Harry!"

He released her and swore loudly and viciously. She backed away from him, hot tears running down her face. Then she turned and ran, stumbling in her haste, from the rose garden.

He stood alone among the roses. He needed a drink. He was not going upstairs to get a jaw-me-dead. He went up to his room by the back stairs and poured himself a glass of brandy from the bottle beside the bed. Gradually he began to relax. He was a prime catch and Mannerling was the prize. Who could turn down Mannerling?

At last, feeling he had not really done anything wrong, he sauntered down to the drawing-room. His mother and father were grim-faced. "The Habards have left," said his mother. "What are we to do with you, Harry? There is no question now of a betrothal. Did you have to paw that girl and frighten her to death?"

"You had better rejoin your regiment," said his father.

Harry walked to the window and looked out across the lawns and flowers to the ornamental lake. He would never leave.

"Forget it," he said over his shoulder. "I'm not going back. And I've already written to my colonel to tell him so."

"I think this place has a curse on it," wailed his mother.

Harry went back to the brandy bottle.

* * *

Lady Beverley was waiting for Robert and Jessica in the garden when they returned. Jessica was talking animatedly about Miss Trumble's efforts to teach them Greek and Latin; her hair was still tousled and her gown displayed, thought Lady Beverley, an unseemly amount of ankle.

"Jessica," she said sharply, "go indoors this minute and change into a more respectable gown and comb your hair. Mr. Sommerville, pray join me. Tea? Wine?"

"Neither, I thank you." He sat down beside her. She was alone; Miss Trumble and the girls were in the house.

"And how go things at Mannerling?" Lady Beverley leaned back in her chair and turned her pale face up to the sun.

"Great excitement today. Harry is to propose to Miss Habard."

She looked for a moment as if he had struck her and then she said faintly, "So all is lost." She had hoped against hope that the gossip should prove to be wrong.

He pretended not to have heard. "Your daughters appear extremely happy here."

She rallied with an obvious effort. "I suppose so. They are young and forget easily."

He was not a man usually given to impulse, but he found himself saying, "I should consider myself highly honoured if you and your family would be my guests at Tarrant Hall."

"What is Tarrant Hall?"

"My home."

"I do not know . . . You are extremely kind. Ah, here is the excellent Miss Trumble."

"I have just suggested to Lady Beverley," said Robert, "that she and her daughters and you, of course, Miss Trumble, might care to visit my home."

"An excellent idea," said Miss Trumble, and then added diplomatically, "Of course it is up to Lady Beverley to decide whether we go or not."

"I do not think so," said Lady Beverley, her brain scrambling this way and that to find any little hope of reclaiming Mannerling. How could she find that hope if they went away?

Barry Wort appeared and said to Miss Trumble, "A moment of your time, madam. Cook seeks your advice."

Only Miss Trumble knew that it was very strange for Barry to interrupt a conversation with a guest for any reason. She rose to her feet and went off with him.

"What is it, Barry?" she asked when they were out of earshot.

"I am friendly with one of the stable lads at Mannerling. I am afraid he is a sad gossip. He rode over from Mannerling a few moments ago, alive with news. Mr. Harry has been spurned by Miss Habard."

"Oh, dear," said Miss Trumble. "They must not learn of this. Mr. Sommerville invited them to stay at his home and I thought it would be marvellous to get them all away from here, and now it is more important than ever that I do. A rejected Harry Devers might come calling. But Lady Beverley will not be moved."

"If I may make a suggestion, ma'am?"

Despite her worry, Miss Trumble smiled. "Do tell me, Barry, for I am at my wits' end."

"You might suggest to my lady that a stay at Mr. Sommerville's would save considerably on bills. It don't be my place to say so, but my lady do be cautious with the pennies."

"You are a genius," exclaimed Miss Trumble. "Oh, I must step into the kitchen to maintain the fiction of advising the cook."

The cook, a retired soldier, Joshua Evans, looked in surprise as Miss Trumble walked into the kitchen, stood counting to ten, and then hurried out again.

Jessica had joined her mother and Robert in the garden. Miss Trumble approached. "My lady, I must beg you to spare me a few minutes. There is a crisis in the kitchen."

"I do not know why I keep servants such as you when I have to deal with matters myself," said Lady Beverley pettishly. Jessica was aware of Robert's face becoming stiff with disapproval and for the first time in her life felt thoroughly ashamed of her mother.

Miss Trumble waited patiently. "Oh, very well," said Lady Beverley.

She went with Miss Trumble to the kitchen, her voice raised in complaint. "What is it *now*?"

When they were inside the cool kitchen with its stone-flagged floor, Miss Trumble said hurriedly, "Do but reconsider Mr. Sommerville's invitation."

"Why should I?"

"A change of air would do you good. Also, there is the saving on household bills here to consider."

Lady Beverley's pale eyes surveyed her governess. "And do you think I am concerned with such petty matters as household economy?"

"Yes, my lady, and I have often admired you for it."

Lady Beverley turned away. Facing her was a large copper pan, burnished to a high shine. As she gazed at it, she could see the distorted reflection of her governess's face. And yet it was not Miss Trumble's face but that of someone she knew or had known. The dim reflection wiped out the lines on Miss Trumble's aged face and an attractive and haughty aristocrat stared out at Lady Beverley from the bottom of the copper pan. She swung back, her mouth a little open in surprise. But it was only Miss Trumble with her wrinkled face and dainty dress, standing staring meekly at the floor.

She thought about what Miss Trumble had said, her mind ranging over the saving on food and candles and laundry.

"I will consider it," she said.

"Perhaps it will be too late," said Miss Trumble. "*He* might have changed his mind."

"And if he has," said Lady Beverley waspishly, "it is because you have kept me too long in my own kitchen."

She hurried out. Miss Trumble suppressed a smile and followed more slowly.

She saw Lady Beverley, looking more animated than she had ever done since Miss Trumble had first met her, talking to Robert.

Safe for a little while, thought Miss Trumble, safe from Mannerling. And now the important thing was to make sure that none of them heard of the rejection of Harry Devers before she got them away.

The girls gathered in Jessica's bedroom that evening after dinner. "So," began Belinda, "what do you think of your Mr. Sommerville, Jessica?"

"Not my Mr. Sommerville," said Jessica, "but he appears very pleasant." She suddenly remembered that kiss and blushed.

"Aha!" cried Abigail. "A tell-tale blush."

"Fiddle," said Jessica. "I am no longer interested in marriage. I may never marry."

"Perhaps Isabella will be the only one of us ever to marry," said Lizzie.

"What can you mean?" cried Rachel.

"Just that everyone seems aware of the fact, except us, that ladies without dowries do not get married. Only look at our Miss Trumble. Sometimes when I look at her I get a sort of picture of the pretty young girl she must have been once."

"Pooh," said Abigail haughtily. "Do not compare any of us with a mere governess."

"Besides," said Rachel, "Mr. Sommerville is not asking all of *us* for the pleasure of our company. It is Jessica he is interested in."

"Would you marry such a man?" asked Lizzie, leaning forward, her long red hair half shielding her face.

"I told you, I am not interested in him as a future husband," said Jessica sharply. "But I do not understand what you mean by saying 'such a man.' He is handsome, comfortably off, and intelligent."

"But he will never have Mannerling."

"Lizzie," pleaded Jessica, "I thought when I told you that Mr. Harry was to marry Miss Habard that we had put hopes of Mannerling behind us. We have been happy, have we not?"

"Perhaps," said Lizzie in a little voice. "Mostly I forget, but I dream a lot, and in my dreams we are all home again and none of this has ever happened."

For once, in their minds, her sisters were of the same mind as Miss Trumble. The sooner they got Lizzie away from the influence of Mannerling, the better.

The date of departure was set for a week later and the girls grew increasingly excited at the prospect of the visit. Robert was to send a carriage for them, a fact that delighted Lady Beverley, who had been beginning to worry about the expense of a post-chaise.

Fortunately for Miss Trumble, Robert had made it very clear that he expected her to be of the party; otherwise Lady Beverley would have made her stay in the role of housekeeper.

On the morning of the day they were to depart, Jessica went in search of Barry and found him feeding the hens.

He eyed her with a certain wariness, hoping she had not heard any news from Mannerling. But it soon became evident that Jessica had heard nothing and was seeking him out to find out if he had.

"Do you know if Mr. Harry is betrothed to Miss Habard?" she asked.

Barry sent up a prayer for forgiveness for the outright lie he was about to tell. "I believe he is, miss."

Jessica felt relief instead of dismay. Just so long as there was no hope left of reclaiming Mannerling, she could forget the place and life could go on.

As they went out to the carriage that had arrived from Tarrant Hall, Barry helped the Sommerville footman and groom load the luggage on the roof. And then, just as Lady Beverley went back into the house to fetch a favourite fan, Barry saw John, the sneaky footman from Mannerling, lounging up the drive, his eyes alight with curiosity. Barry moved forward to stop him from approaching any nearer.

"You're trespassing," said Barry. "Off with you."

John ignored him. "Where are that lot off to, then?" he asked. "I was riding past on my road back from Hedgefield and saw the carriage."

"Be off with you," hissed Barry. "You've no business here."

"I worked as footman for Lady Beverley. I'm sure my lady will want to say good day to me."

Barry looked at him in a fury. He did not want the gossiping John to know that the Beverleys were going to Tarrant Hall. He did not want them anywhere near the family in case he told them about Harry's rejection.

John strolled past him with an insolent sneer on his face. Barry seized his arm and twisted it up his back and marched him back down the drive to where his horse was tethered to a tree. He gave him a final shove towards it. "Mount," he growled, "or I'll draw your cork."

John looked at Barry's pugnacious face and quickly threw himself up into the saddle. Feeling safer, he leaned down. "There's something going on here," he said. "I'll find out what it is." He suddenly lashed out at Barry's face with his riding crop, but Barry nimbly jumped back. John wheeled his horse and set off at a smart canter. Barry shook his worried head. He would need to warn the remaining servants not to gossip. Then he returned to make his goodbyes to the Beverleys. No doubt Robert Sommerville would tell them about Mr. Harry, but by that time they would be safe in his home.

Fortunately for Barry, Harry Devers was in London, so John, the footman, was unable to seek him out and tell him about the odd goings-on at Brookfield House. Harry was surfacing from a heavy drunken sleep when his man awoke him to tell him that his friend, Captain Gully Fawcett, had called.

"Good old Gully," said Harry. "Show him up and get me a seltzer. Oh, my head."

Gully sloped into the room. He was a tall, thin man with a weak face and pale eyes.

"You look a wreck," he said amiably.

"Roistering until dawn," said Harry.

"You were calling toasts all night to some female called Jessica Beverley."

"I was?"

"Fairest creature in England, you kept saying."

"Some impoverished local lady," said Harry. "But, begad, I had forgot how beautiful she was. Better than that silly little fat-eyed Habard female."

"The one who turned you down?"

Harry glared at him furiously for a moment and then said ruefully, "I seem to have been babbling on."

"What I want to know," said Gully, sitting down on the end of the bed, "is what are you doing in London if this fair charmer is in the country?"

"She'll keep," said Harry. "I can have that one any time I please."

"But not outside marriage?"

"No."

"Won't your parents have something to say on that score? I never knew parents yet who were prepared to give their blessing to a marriage where no or little money was involved."

"Oh, they'll howl a bit, but then they'll let me have what I want. They always do."

"Thought they were going to cut off your funds because you're leaving the army."

"They huff and puff a bit, but they always come around. I tell you what I'm missing. I'm missing Mannerling."

"Who's she?"

"Not she. My home in the country. Bless me, you've never seen anywhere so beautiful."

"Beautiful home, beautiful Miss Beverley. I repeat, why are you here?"

"Because both of 'em ain't going to run away. I need a bit of fun without my parents breathing down my neck. There's the Cyprian ball at the Argyll Rooms tonight. If I don't die before then."

The Beverleys had assumed that Robert Sommerville lived alone. But it transpired that his sister Honoria resided with him. She was a spinster in her late thirties. Like her brother she was tall, black-haired, and black-eyed. The strong features that made her brother handsome made her look formidable. But she certainly appeared all that was amiable as she welcomed them, and the sisters saw nothing to fear.

Tarrant Hall was a comfortable mansion set in rolling parkland. It had every elegance and comfort. The rooms allocated to each were well-appointed, the servants were polite and efficient, and the cook was excellent. Away from the spell of Mannerling, the girls chattered happily, enjoying this unexpected holiday. Robert Sommerville had said nothing about Harry Devers, and no one had asked him for any news.

Only the shrewd Miss Trumble sensed trouble ahead. She alone had not been deceived by the amiable Miss Honoria Sommerville. Miss Trumble quickly came to the conclusion that Honoria enjoyed being mistress of Tarrant Hall and had no intention of relinquishing her position by letting her brother marry.

Miss Trumble could only rely on the obvious strength of Robert's character and the hope that he could not be influenced by this sister of his. She began to relax as the days passed and Robert and Jessica talked together, went for walks, and spent a great deal of time in each other's company.

Honoria watched and waited and bided her time. To point out to her brother that the Beverleys had no money to speak of would not affect him, for had he not told her that fact himself?

She studied the sisters. Miss Trumble, she reflected, was the problem. Despite the fact they were all on a visit, the governess continued to educate the girls each morning and Robert often joined in these schoolroom sessions, confiding to his sister that it was a pleasure to find girls who were intelligent as well as beautiful. Honoria led–usually–a calm, self-sufficient life. She was not used to making friends, particularly among younger members of her own sex. But she realized she would have to get close to one of them if she was to find out some weakness, or piece of gossip, she could exploit.

It was then her attention was drawn to little Lizzie. There was something sad at the back of the girl's eyes and she did not seem as carefree as her sisters. Nor was she as beautiful, being cursed with red hair.

There was a lake in the grounds and Honoria found out by diligent questioning of the servants that Lizzie was in the habit of retreating there in the afternoons. Armed one day with a piece of petit point, she made her way to the lake. Sure enough, Lizzie was sitting there on a bench at the edge of the water, a book lying on her lap. The girl was not reading, Honoria noticed, but looking out across the water. She sat down beside her after murmuring a quiet "Good day," and began to sew.

Lizzie picked up her book and rose to her feet. "No, do not run away," said Honoria. "I shall sit here and sew and leave you to your meditations."

Lizzie sat down again reluctantly. The sun shone and a little breeze ruffled the waters of the lake. Somewhere in the grounds a peacock screamed suddenly, its harsh cry rending the pastoral stillness, and then all was quiet again.

"We had peacocks at Mannerling," said Lizzie half to herself.

"Mannerling? Our relatives, the Deverses, live there. I have been invited several times but I prefer it here," said Honoria, placidly stitching away at a fat rose.

"Oh, but you should go." Now Honoria had Lizzie's full attention. Lizzie wanted to talk about Mannerling. It nagged and nagged away at her, but her sisters now shied away from the very mention of the place. "We lived there," said Lizzie, "until Papa lost all the money."

There was a yearning note in her voice. Honoria entered another neat stitch. "Tell me about it, my child."

"It is hard to explain," said Lizzie eagerly. "It is very graceful, the building, you know, and the painted ceilings are a glorious riot of colour. It enfolds you in its quiet peace. We thought Isabella, my eldest sister, would marry Mr. Judd, the new owner, but he married Mary Stoppard, the vicar's daughter, a little nobody, and then he hanged himself."

The busy needle paused. "Dear me, why did he do that?"

"You see, he lost his money, too, and how could anyone live without Mannerling?"

"Your elder sister married Lord Fitzpatrick, did she not?"

"Yes, although she could have made a push and secured Mr. Judd."

"But, my child, if your sister had married Mr. Judd, she would have been an impoverished widow with a tragedy in her background. Would you wish her to endure that?"

"I am sure she could have stopped him from gambling."

"How did your papa lose his money?"

"Gambling," said Lizzie in a low voice.

"But neither you, your sisters, nor Lady Beverley were evidently able to do anything about that."

"We did not know about it until it was too late."

"Then I think the same thing could be said about the undistinguished vicar's daughter. Hardened gamblers cannot be stopped."

Lizzie bent her head. Honoria's black eyes were hard and shrewd as she surveyed that bent head. "My cousin Harry is a bachelor," she said meditatively, "and he is the heir to Mannerling."

"He told Mr. Sommerville that he was going to propose to Jessica and Mr. Sommerville came to warn Jessica to have nothing to do with him."

Honoria, who loathed Harry, said with affected surprise, "I wonder why he did that? Harry is a bit wild, but gay and handsome. All he needs is a wife to settle him down."

"He has found one," said Lizzie.

"You amaze me! There has been no announcement in the newspapers. Mrs. Devers would most certainly have written to me should such an event have occurred. To whom is he betrothed?"

"A Miss Habard."

"I think you must be mistaken, but I shall write to Mannerling and find out. I am not in the way of gossiping, Miss Lizzie, and my brother would be angry if he found out, so do not say anything of this."

"My family would be angry with me as well. Do you . . . do you think your brother will marry Jessica?"

Over my dead body, thought Honoria. But she said aloud, "They make a handsome couple, I admit. But Robert is a confirmed bachelor. From time to time he invites some pretty lady and her family here, but it never comes to anything. Shall we return to the house for tea?"

Happy to have found a friend, Lizzie trotted beside her.

From an upstairs window, Miss Trumble watched their approach and frowned. She did not trust Honoria.

"I have never climbed an apple tree in my life before," Jessica called down to Robert, who was standing underneath the tree laughing up at her.

"So what made you do it now, my hoyden?"

"A sudden impulse," said Jessica. "I never act on impulse. Perhaps this is how Isabella felt."

"When? What did she do?"

"Isabella was the stateliest and proudest of us all, and yet one day when we were on a call to the vicarage, she suddenly left and a farmer told us later he had seen her running and running through the woods and across the fields."

He held up his arms. "I will help you down."

Jessica slid down into his arms. He held her close and looked down into her flushed face. "Jessica," he said.

And then, behind him, he heard his sister's voice. "Robert! Tea is served!"

He released Jessica, but then drew her arm through his and walked past his sister towards the house. Honoria stood for a moment looking after them. Something would have to be done, and quickly, too.

She joined the rest for tea but excused herself as quickly as possible. She went to her private sitting-room and began to write to Mrs. Devers, asking if the news of Harry's betrothal was true. She added that Robert was entertaining the Beverleys. Then she changed into a carriage dress and was driven to the nearest town, where she sent the letter express and paid for a reply by express post as well.

Mrs. Devers's reply was prompt. Harry had ruined any chance of a betrothal to Miss Habard, an excellent dowry, too, and had taken himself off to London. He was obsessed with Mannerling and had sold out of the army. He was shortly expected home. Mrs. Devers warned Honoria against encouraging any marital hopes among the Beverleys. Jessica Beverley had made her pursuit of Harry and her ambitions vulgarly obvious to all.

Honoria read the letter several times. She was tempted to show it to Robert and then decided against it. Instead she made her way to the lake and found Lizzie on her usual bench. Forcing herself to be quiet and calm, Honoria encouraged Lizzie to talk about her favourite subject, Mannerling, and then said idly, "I had a letter from Mrs. Devers. Harry Devers is not engaged to anyone. He turned down Miss Habard. It seems that he was too much taken up with Miss Jessica." Honoria told this lie without a qualm. "He has been in London but is expected back shortly."

She had the satisfaction of seeing the wide-eyed expression of shock and then dawning hope on Lizzie's little face.

"You must excuse me," said Lizzie in a stifled voice. "I have forgotten something in the house.

Honoria watched her go and then smiled to herself.

Lizzie called "a council of war." It could not take place until they were all supposed to have retired to bed, for somehow Miss Trumble sensed that something was in the air and was always in their company, her eyes darting from one face to the other.

They gathered in Jessica's bedroom, sitting crouched on her bed, the room lit only by one candle, and with a blanket stuffed along the bottom of the door so that Miss Trumble, should she be passing, might not enter to demand why the light was still shining.

"What is it, Lizzie?" asked Jessica.

"I have such news," said Lizzie eagerly. "Miss Sommerville talks to me quite a lot. She said she had a letter from Mrs. Devers, and Harry has turned down Miss Habard."

"That is an odd way of putting it," said Abigail slowly.

"Surely Miss Habard did not propose to *him*?"

"Oh, that is no matter. According to Mrs. Devers, Harry did not want to marry Miss Habard because he is too interested in our Jessica. There!"

There were no claps or cries of joy.

"And he is expected back from London soon," said Lizzie, now in a pleading voice. "Don't you see? We should be there."

They all looked at Jessica. Jessica wondered if a soldier felt like this when he had a brief respite from the war in some pretty village and then found he was being ordered back into battle. She thought of Robert. She knew his feelings towards her had been becoming warmer each day and she had done nothing to discourage him. And yet, she owed it to her sisters to reclaim their old home if she could.

"We have been happy here," she said in a low voice.

"You will not be like Isabella," begged Lizzie. "You always said you would never be like Isabella. Is it Robert? Is that why you are not delighted, Jessica?"

"I don't know what to think," said Jessica wretchedly. "Let us ask Mama."

"She will be asleep," protested Rachel.

"We will see" was all Jessica would say.

Taking the blanket away from the door and looking round it cautiously first, in case the vigilant Miss Trumble might be watching, they crept quietly along the corridor to Lady Beverley's room.

Lady Beverley was sitting up in bed, reading a fashion journal. She looked up in surprise as her daughters stole quietly into the room.

She listened carefully as Lizzie told her the news.

"There is only one thing we can do now," she said firmly. "We must return home immediately."

"Must we?" asked Jessica. "Will it not be considered very odd to leave so abruptly?"

"I will say I have not been well," said Lady Beverley. "Oh, my darling child. Such news! Now we have happiness to look forward to."

But Jessica had a nagging feeling that she was leaving happiness behind.

Chapter Five

The game's afoot:
Follow your spirit; and, upon this charge
Cry "God for Harry! England and Saint
George!"

—*William Shakespeare*

The hunt was up. There was an almost feverish anticipation about the Beverley girls as they made preparations for their departure from Tarrant Hall.

Robert Sommerville, hard-eyed, had learned from his sister that Lady Beverley was "poorly," and must needs return to the care of her own physician.

He did not believe Lady Beverley was in ill health. He was sure something had occurred to reanimate the ambitions of Jessica and her family. Somehow, they must have learned the news, and only the night before, that Harry Devers was still on the marriage market, and yet he had been vain enough, he chided himself, to begin to think that it was because of him that Jessica had forgotten Mannerling.

Before he even saw Jessica he could hear the girls' excitement and laughter as they supervised their packing. To say he was disappointed in Jessica was putting it mildly. He thought her contemptible.

And then Lady Beverley called on him in his study, holding her smelling salts, and putting on an act of being at death's door, which irritated him further.

But he agreed she must leave immediately, and with every appearance of calm accepted her apologies and her thanks.

But no sooner had she left than he hurled his coffee cup across the room and swore loudly. He would not stay to say goodbye to Jessica Beverley. He never wanted to see her again.

He went upstairs, changed into his riding-clothes, and walked over to the stables. The day was fine, with only a hint of cold heralding approaching autumn. A beautiful morning for riding. But the glory of the morning only seemed to intensify the blackness in his heart. He mounted his horse and rode off, planning to return when he was sure they had gone. What shoddy, greedy people, he raged inwardly.

Honoria watched her brother ride off, a satisfied little smile curving her lips. It was she who went out to the front of the house to wave goodbye. She noticed with added satisfaction that Jessica accepted the intelligence that Robert was out riding with a sort of hard calm. Honoria made Lizzie a fond farewell, feeling quite tender towards the little girl who had been unwittingly so helpful.

It was a cheerful and happy family who were driven off from Tarrant Hall. Only Jessica began to feel sad as the carriage left the drive and moved along the country road that started the journey home. Clouds were beginning to cover the sun and a few leaves fluttered down from the trees. She had woken that morning hard and determined to fulfil her family's ambitions. But as the carriage rolled ever homewards and the day grew darker, she began to feel a creeping shame. An intelligent man like Robert Sommerville had surely not been taken in by Lady Beverley's bad acting. He would think them rude and ungrateful. But at least, Jessica tried to comfort herself, he had not seemed to know that Harry was not engaged. But his sister did! So she would tell him, if she had not already done so, and he would realize why they had left and despise them heartily for it.

Suddenly Miss Trumble said, "Miss Sommerville was happy to see us go . . . almost triumphant. One could believe she had engineered our departure herself. But that is ridiculous, is it not, Lizzie?"

"Quite ridiculous," said Lady Beverley roundly. "I am, in fact, quite fatigued. I shall be glad to get to our own home."

Lizzie bit her lip and then shook her head so that her two wings of red hair shielded her face from Miss Trumble's bright gaze.

Jessica felt a pang of dread. She had begun to sense that Honoria disapproved of Robert's interest in her. What if Miss Sommerville had made the whole thing up to get rid of them?

Robert rode wearily back towards Tarrant Hall. He was not only ashamed of Jessica but ashamed of his own warm feelings towards the girl. He was like any other fool of a man, seeing sterling qualities that did not exist, and all because of a pretty face and a well-turned ankle.

As Tarrant Hall came into view across the fields, he slowed his horse to an amble as a thought suddenly struck him. He had been so sure that no one at Tarrant Hall had known any news from Mannerling. He had carefully not told Honoria. He had a sudden sharp memory of Jessica smiling down at him from the apple tree. And then he had lifted her down. How close he had been to kissing her. How very close he had been to losing his heart. And then Honoria had interrupted them and for a moment he had thought she had looked like a wardress, standing there in the sunlight, her arms folded.

For the first time, he began to wonder about Honoria. For the first time he realized what her position would be in the house if he married. She would either have to take second place to his wife, and he could not now imagine Honoria taking second place to anyone, or she would need to find somewhere else to live.

He spurred his weary horse, suddenly anxious to confront

his sister. But Honoria looked genuinely surprised when he asked her whether she had told any of the Beverleys about Harry's failed engagement. "I did not even know Harry was about to propose to anyone," exclaimed Honoria. "And what should such intelligence have to do with the Beverleys' abrupt departure?"

But that Robert was not prepared to tell her.

Harry Devers arrived back at Mannerling. He was feeling fit and well, having drunk nothing stronger than chocolate and seltzer for the past few days. He walked from room to room, noticing, he felt for the first time, the full beauty and grace of the place. His enjoyment was interrupted by John, the footman.

"What is it?" demanded Harry.

"The Beverleys are returned, sir."

"Oh, them. And what's that to do with me?"

"I beg your pardon, sir," said John, backing away.

"Wait a bit. Returned from where?"

"From visiting Mr. Robert Sommerville."

Harry scowled, but said with seeming indifference, "Leave me."

After John had left, Harry walked through the Long Gallery. The Beverley ancestors had been taken down and replaced with the Deverses' ancestors. A few painted faces, much like his own, stared indifferently down at him.

Robert must be after Jessica, he thought savagely. He should have questioned John further. Jessica might be engaged. No time was to be lost. He would be careful this time. No grabbing, no kissing. He would go carefully. He hurried up the stairs, shouting for his man to come and barber him, and shouting for someone to fetch his carriage round to the front door.

It was an uncharacteristically quiet and soberly dressed Harry Devers who called on the Beverleys. He was struck anew by Jessica's beauty. And she loved Mannerling as much as he. In his mind, he saw the grand parties he would give at Mannerling, with the ornament of Jessica at his side. But he carefully did not suggest any walks in the garden and set himself to entertain the Beverley family with descriptions of the plays he had never seen but had read about in the newspapers. He had not had time to go to the playhouse, what with all the wenching and drinking.

Jessica felt the little pain at her heart, which had been there since she left Tarrant Hall, finally leaving her. Harry was so good-looking and amiable. Lizzie suggested a game of loo and her sisters quickly pooh-poohed the idea, but Harry said indulgently that he would enjoy playing and joined in the game with such enthusiasm that perhaps only the cynical Miss Trumble suspected that the pennies Harry was winning were transferred in his imagination into thousands of pounds.

When he finally took his leave, the sisters vowed it had been a capital evening. Harry, driving home, was well satisfied with the evening as well, although he considered such entertainment beneath him, but it had given him a chance to ingratiate himself with Jessica, to admire the swell of her bosom and the shine of her hair. No need to rush things. When they were married, he could do exactly what he liked with her. He passed the rest of the journey home dreaming of just that.

In the following weeks, as summer gave way to winter, Harry was a frequent and welcome caller. Miss Trumble felt powerless to do anything to stop the inevitable from happening, the inevitable being his engagement to Jessica.

As for Jessica, she had practically forgotten Robert Sommerville. She now fancied herself in love with Harry and gave him virtues and intelligence that he did not possess. There was only one cloud in her life, and that was that neither she nor the rest of her family were ever invited to Mannerling.

This was something that was beginning to irritate Harry, and when he learned that they were to hold another ball and that the Beverleys had not been invited, he complained to his parents.

"You may as well face up to it," he said harshly, "I am going to marry Jessica Beverley."

"Not suitable," said his father angrily. "No money there, and the girl has no interest in you. She only wants Mannerling."

"And she'll have it," said Harry brutally. "I don't want either of you around when I get wed."

"You may have forgotten," said Mr. Devers, outraged, "that this is my home."

"I'm your heir. I get this place when you die, so you may as well let me have it now. If you don't do what I want, I'll make your lives a misery."

"It's this curst place!" wailed Mrs. Devers. "You used to be such a sweet boy . . ." she cried, thus carefully forgetting all the scandals her son had been embroiled in.

"And you can start by asking the Beverleys to your damned ball. I'll announce the engagement then. You stand in my way, and it will be the worse for you." He loomed over his cringing parents, a mad look in his eyes.

"Something will stop you from this folly. *I* will stop you," said his mother, beginning to sob.

Mr. Devers shifted uneasily in his chair after Harry had stormed out. He was beginning to hate Mannerling. He thought it was like living in a museum where everything was cherished and polished. He wanted a real home again where he could come in from hunting and sit with his muddy clothes and with his boots on by the fire instead of rushing upstairs to be changed and groomed as if he, too, were a statue or objet d'art, to be carefully polished up to be worthy of his surroundings. Harry would surely settle down once he was wed. Jessica Beverley was no serving wench. She was of good family. He felt weakly that to make life comfortable again, it might be as well to give Harry what he wanted. It had always made life comfortable in the past to give Harry just what he wanted.

He and his wife discussed the problem in low voices. They could, he said, find a tidy property of their own, far from Mannerling, and let Harry get on with it. If they did not, they would risk losing the love of their only son, for both Mr. and Mrs. Devers really believed that Harry loved them, that he was young and wild, but nothing worse.

And so a triumphant Harry was told that he might have both Jessica and Mannerling.

"I suppose you will ride over to Lady Beverley and obtain her permission," said his mother bleakly.

"Don't need to," retorted Harry. "Big surprise announcement is what we want."

"As you like," said his father wearily. "At least you will not meet with a refusal. Imagine any Beverley turning down a chance of getting their claws on Mannerling."

John, the footman, who had heard much of the debate between Mr. and Mrs. Devers, was alarmed at the thought of Jessica's becoming mistress of Mannerling. He had worked for the Beverleys and, after their downfall, had enjoyed being insolent to them. He knew he would probably lose his job. On the pretext of running an errand, he made his way down to the village and so to the vicarage, where he found Mary Judd cutting late flowers in the garden. He leaned on the garden gate and gave her a good day.

"And how go things at Mannerling, John?" asked Mary with an air of hauteur which she hoped counteracted the fact that she was pumping this servant for gossip.

"Badly, madam," said John. "Mr. Harry is going to announce his engagement to Miss Jessica Beverley at the ball."

Mary's eyes were as hard as stones. The highest point in her life had been when Ajax Judd had announced his engagement to herself, not to one of the Beverleys. How she had enjoyed their mortification and their hatred of seeing her ruling the roost at Mannerling. But then Judd had committed suicide, and here she was again in the vicarage, her only comfort being that the Beverleys were not invited to Mannerling, whereas she herself was.

"I never thought to see the day," mourned John. "I thought Miss Jessica would have married Mr. Robert."

"Mr. Robert Sommerville. How so?"

"The Beverleys were all at his place, Tarrant Hall, on an extended visit."

"Are you sure?"

"Yes, and very hush-hush it all was, too. I got it out of one of the housemaids. She had been warned not to say anything by that Barry, who is only an odd man and not even an upper servant."

"The Beverleys have no upper servants," said Mary with sour satisfaction.

"I wonder," said John, looking at the sky, "what Mr. Robert would say if he knew."

"He'll know soon enough." Mary decapitated a late rose. "The announcement will be in the newspapers."

"Ah, but that's it. The announcement isn't going to be made until the night of the ball. He ain't . . . isn't even going to ask Lady Beverley for her permission."

"Well, he hardly needs to do that. He knows they will jump at any offer."

Mary saw a neighbour coming down the road. She must remember what was due to her position as a former mistress of Mannerling. "Be off with you," she snapped. "I do not like servants' gossip."

John went on his way feeling comforted. Mary Judd would do something to spike the Beverleys' guns if anyone could.

Robert Sommerville subsequently received a letter from Mary Judd. At first he could not remember who she was and then he placed her in his mind as the vicar's daughter, an encroaching and oily sort of female. The news that Harry was to announce his engagement to Jessica at the ball came as no surprise to him. He decided not to attend the ball himself. The only thing that nagged at his mind was how the Beverleys had found out that Harry was still free to wed. Although he frequently told himself that such as Jessica Beverley was not worth a thought, he nonetheless had diligently questioned the servants. He believed them when they told him that they had heard no news, and furthermore, that Lady Beverley never talked to any of them except to issue orders, and that went for her daughters as well.

"Who is the letter from?" asked Honoria. They were seated at the breakfast table.

"Someone I once knew," he said. "No one of interest." He did not want to discuss the Beverleys with Honoria.

"Have you heard from the Beverleys?" she asked.

"No, why?"

"I thought they might have communicated with us."

He was suddenly suspicious of her. He had been more aware of her since the departure of Jessica and her family than he had ever been, wondering again whether Honoria would resent his getting married. He tried to put Jessica out of his mind, but when he saw his sister go out driving to make calls, on a sudden impulse, he went to her study. All was tidy and neat and very unfeminine, more like a man's room. He went to the writing-desk in the corner. There was a leather-bound diary lying on top of it.

Feeling very low and mean, he opened it and began to read, but there was nothing in its pages except reminders of what to order, which servant to speak to, and whom she was due to call on. But having stooped so low, he could not leave it there. He studied her desk and then opened the drawers. Neat sheets of parchment, a bottle of ink, sealing-wax and seals, household accounts, bills, nothing of importance to him. And then he wondered if the desk had a secret drawer such as the one in his own, which was a compartment at the back of the top right-hand drawer.

He pulled the top right-hand drawer out to its fullest, and sure enough, there was the compartment. In it was a letter. He took it out and sat down and read it. It was from Mrs. Devers, and she was all too obviously replying to a letter from Honoria. And in it there was the intelligence of how Harry was not engaged to Miss Habard. He slowly replaced the letter and closed the drawer. The letter was dated two days before the Beverleys' abrupt departure.

He remembered thinking that his sister's friendship with little Lizzie was somehow touching. Now he thought he saw it all. Honoria had told Lizzie, Lizzie had told her sisters and mother, and they had all hurried off to try to secure the prize. It could be argued that Honoria had therefore saved him from making a cake of himself over a girl who could never have any affection for him at all.

And yet, he remembered once inviting a Miss Ranken and her parents to stay. Miss Ranken had been a jolly, pretty, uncomplicated sort of girl, and although his affections had not been seriously engaged, he had begun to think of proposing to her and ending his bachelor state. Honoria had been very cordial to Miss Ranken, he remembered. And then one day the Rankens had departed just as hurriedly as the Beverleys.

He felt trapped. He wanted to confront Honoria with the evidence but could not bring himself to admit that he had searched her desk. But he could no longer live with her.

He went to the window and looked out. Tarrant Hall was a pleasant place, but he had lived in it for only a few years. There were no family ties. He was a rich man. If Honoria wanted to remain at Tarrant Hall, then let her have the place. He would buy another estate, nearer the university, and never, ever would she be allowed to meddle in his life again.

Unaware of the changes that were about to beset her,

Honoria changed into a taffeta gown and went down to join her brother for dinner. She talked of the calls she had made and how old Mrs. Johnson, who had been ill for some months, had been faring, while the servants came and went with various dishes. Then she made to rise. "I will leave you to your wine."

"Stay," he commanded. "Sit down and listen to me. I am tired of Tarrant Hall."

"But why?"

"That is my concern. You like it here, do you not?"

"Indeed, yes, brother. I have a very pleasant life."

"It is as I thought. I am making you a present of Tarrant Hall, Honoria."

"But what is this? Are you going away?"

"I have a desire to set up my own establishment."

"But you will need me! You cannot do without me. I am your hostess. I am–"

"My wife will perform those functions."

"Your wife? Jessica Beverley?"

"Not Jessica Beverley nor any other female I have in mind at the moment. It is better this way. You can continue to hold sway here."

Honoria looked at him in dismay. It would not be at all the same. It was Robert who had all the friends. She had never troubled to make any of her own. She would lead a very solitary life. Of course the local county would come to call, but a spinster would not be invited to many places, whereas a sister and marriageable brother were.

"Who wrote to you?" she demanded.

"That is my business. Now you may leave me to my wine."

Honoria felt quite weak and shaky.

"By the way, remember I told you to refuse the invitations to the Mannerling ball?"

"Yes."

"Have you sent that letter?"

"I was going to write it this evening."

"Don't. Accept instead."

"But I do not wish to go! I never want to go to Mannerling. Harry Devers is a lout."

"Agreed. You do not need to go. I shall accept."

Honoria stared at him. It was something to do with Jessica Beverley. She must go with him.

"On the other hand," she said with affected casualness, "it might be amusing to see this mansion which so obsesses the Beverleys."

"And how do you know it so obsesses the Beverleys?"

"Something the youngest said. Brother, I must tell you, Jessica Beverley is not for you."

"I know that. Her engagement to Harry Devers is to be announced at the ball."

"Then why . . . ? Oh, no matter," said Honoria, still feeling weak and shaken. He must have somehow found out about her letter to Mrs. Devers. That must have been in the letter he received. She suddenly hated Jessica Beverley from the bottom of her heart. The girl might be obsessed with Mannerling, but her normally calm, sensible, and intelligent brother was obsessed with *her*!

Miss Trumble escaped from the excitement of the invitations to the ball and sought out Barry. "The thing that worries me, Barry," she said with a sigh, "is that I cannot help having a feeling that Honoria Sommerville engineered the whole thing. I hate that woman."

"That would be Mr. Robert's sister. How could she do that?"

"She befriended Lizzie, a most uncharacteristic thing for her to do–I am persuaded of that. She was talking to Lizzie by the lake at Tarrant Hall the day before our departure. Lizzie told them something, something that excited them all, and then they said they must return because Lady Beverley was ill, and yet, you must admit, she has never been in better spirits."

"It is a pity," said Barry. "Robert Sommerville is a fine man."

"If Jessica marries Harry Devers, I really think I will give up my post here and return home."

"And where is home, miss?"

"Oh, not that far away," said Miss Trumble vaguely.

"It would be a pity to abandon the others to their fate."

"I do not think anything can be done with them." Miss Trumble kicked at the grass with her shoe.

"I thought the same about Miss Isabella, but she married a fine man."

"We'll see" was all Miss Trumble would say.

Barry watched her slim upright figure as she walked away. There was a mystery about Miss Trumble. He knew from gossip that her references had never arrived. He wondered who she really was. He hoped she would not leave. If she did, he would be tempted to take up Isabella's, Lady Fitzpatrick's, offer and go to join her household in Ireland. He wished from the bottom of his heart that the Beverley girls were as wise as they were beautiful.

Chapter Six

We make guilty of our disasters the sun, the moon, and the stars; as if we were villains by necessity, fools by heavenly compulsion.

—WILLIAM SHAKESPEARE

Jessica paced nervously up and down the garden as the day of the ball approached, increasingly nervous, increasingly ill at ease, her hair brushed loosely down about her shoulders. She was not expecting Harry to call. His last call had been on the Wednesday of the week before. He had said he would be busy right up until the ball. He had been warm and affectionate and she had felt happy and secure when he left. But contrary to what she had been told, absence did not seem to be making the heart grow fonder. What Robert had told her of Harry's character began to worry her for the first time, and besides, she had begun to dream of Robert, sensuous, languorous dreams that no lady should have. She began to feel haunted by Robert Sommerville. She was beginning to have a wish, which she kept trying to drive out of her head, that Harry would not propose to her. Had not Isabella at that fatal ball at Mannerling been so sure that Mr. Judd would propose to her? And had not he humiliated her by proposing to Mary Stoddard?

But Lord Fitzpatrick had been deeply in love with Isabella and had forgiven her for her pursuit of Judd. That she, Jessica, might have made her ambitions regarding Mannerling plain enough and vulgar enough to be instrumental in spoiling any chance she might have had with Robert was something she preferred not to think about. She tried to tell herself that her duty lay with Mannerling and with Harry Devers, and to fight down any weak thought that if she escaped marriage to him, life might be pleasant again. She could not confide in Miss Trumble, but at last did tell her sisters of her doubts. Belinda said firmly—and the others agreed—that her nerves were understandable. She was merely frightened that she might undergo the same treatment as Mr. Judd had meted out to Isabella.

"It's a little like bride nerves, I think," said Lizzie with a quaint air of wisdom. "And only think, Jessica! You will be home again."

That lifted Jessica's spirits, but that night she dreamt of Robert again and awoke with tears streaming down her face, for in her dream he had come to Mannerling and she was married to Harry and Robert had stared at her with contempt and said, "I told you you would be miserable."

Then the time began to hurtle by as everyone except Jessica and Miss Trumble fretted over what she should wear to secure the affections of Harry. Jessica insisted on wearing a simple white ball gown that she had worn only once before. It was high-waisted and flounced at the hem in the current fashion. Miss Trumble surprised her by presenting her with a rich and gaudy Indian shawl, all reds and golds. It was soft and warm, rich and dramatic. It was obviously a very expensive gift, but Miss Trumble said quietly that her previous employer had been very generous. "Who was your previous employer?" asked Jessica.

"Yes, I think that shawl becomes you," said Miss Trumble. "I have a painted fan that would go very well with it."

"Have you noticed," asked Belinda when their governess had left the room, "that she never talks about her previous employ, nor has she given Mama any references? I do hope there is nothing sinister in our Miss Trumble's past."

"I doubt it," said Jessica. "I cannot see the correct Miss Trumble doing anything wrong. I wish I could talk to her about Mr. Harry."

Belinda looked alarmed. "You must not! She does not approve. She would try to persuade you to allow Mr. Sommerville to court you."

"After our departure from Tarrant Hall and Mama's obvious lie about being ill, I doubt very much Mr. Sommerville wants to see any of us again." And with that, Jessica burst into tears.

Belinda looked at her weeping sister in exasperation. "Never tell me you have formed a tendre for Mr. Sommerville! It is the outside of enough. First Isabella, and now you."

Jessica dried her eyes and said shakily, "It is nothing. I am simply worried that I shall fail."

Belinda's face cleared and she gave her a fierce hug. "You will not fail."

And after Belinda had left, Jessica thought gloomily that she had sounded exactly like Lady Macbeth.

Once more to Mannerling, nervous, hopeful, and excited. Miss Trumble had never voiced the full extent of her disapproval aloud, but it was obvious to all the Beverleys that she considered Harry Devers not a suitable gentleman, and so she had been left behind. So, too, had Barry, for this time the Mannerling coach, coachman, and footmen had been sent to convey the Beverleys, a mark of distinction that made Lady Beverley begin to relax. Nothing could go wrong this time. Mannerling was as good as theirs.

Miss Trumble waved them goodbye and walked around the back of the house in search of Barry. She found him sitting on an old kitchen chair, smoking a clay pipe. He stood up when he saw her. "They've gone?"

"Yes, Barry, and I would dearly like to have gone with them this time. I keep praying that Harry Devers has put his wild past behind him. I also keep hoping that there is some fair heiress there to take his attention."

"Reckon us might be able to have a look," said Barry.

"How so?"

"They've gone off in the Mannerling coach. We could take out the carriage and horse from the stable here and ride over."

"And then what? Turn up at the ball arm in arm?"

"You joke, miss. No, we could leave the carriage with the others. The Mannerling servants will be too busy to bother about us. We could go round by the back stairs and up to the musicians' gallery. They'll be playing and won't pay us much heed. We could stand at the back of the band and watch the dancing."

"You are sure that Lady Beverley will not see us?"

"It is a cold night. Take a warm wrap for her and leave it with the ladies' cloaks. That's in a little room off the great hall. Then if asked, you can say you were concerned that she might be too cold on the journey home and brought the shawl and left it downstairs with Betty, and then, as you were at Mannerling, decided to discreetly view the dancing."

"You seem remarkably well informed as to the geography of Mannerling, Barry."

"I got to know the house well when the Deverses first took up residence, for my lady was always sending me over there with some gift. Then the servants were as proud of the house as their masters and took me around and bragged about how fine everything was."

"Then we shall try."

"We'll treat it like a military campaign, miss."

"Ah," said Miss Trumble, "you have forgot that at least in any military campaign there is hope of success."

For the first time in her life, the magic of Mannerling failed to reach Jessica as she mounted the staircase to the chain of saloons that formed the ballroom. Mrs. Devers surveyed her with cold eyes, Mr. Devers wearily. Harry beamed at her as she curtsied low. Jessica moved on into the ballroom. Her eyes flew immediately to Robert Sommerville's handsome face. And then an odd thing happened. It seemed as if his face was bright, lit from within, and that the rest of the ballroom and guests had faded into a vague greyness. He bowed slightly and turned and walked away and all the noise and chatter of the ballroom came flooding back.

She looked around her and then up to the painted ceilings, to the rollicking gods and goddesses. If she played her cards right, all this would soon be hers again. "Not yours," said a voice in her head, "always your husband's. A woman has no say in anything."

But soon Harry was at her side, asking for a dance. Harry was very sober. He did not want to be humiliated again, the way he had been by that fool of a Habard girl. His predatory eyes covertly took inventory of every charm of Jessica's body that he could see, and he dreamt lecherously of the bits that he could not. Jessica thought only of Mannerling, wondering why the fascination the house held for her should have suddenly deserted her. The evening dragged on. She was always aware of Robert, of his partners, waiting always for him to approach, but he did not. His sister, Honoria, was there. Lizzie had gone up to speak to her, but Honoria had been dismissive. Lizzie had served her purpose. The little girl bored her now.

And then, just before the supper dance, there was a roll of drums. Mr. Devers held up his hands for silence. "My son has an important announcement to make," he said.

Harry took his place. Up in the musicians' gallery, Miss Trumble sent up a prayer. Barry stood beside her, a comforting and solid figure.

"My lords, ladies and gentlemen," said Harry proudly. "I wish to announce my engagement. But I must tell you, I have not yet asked the lady to marry me."

There was a buzz of excitement. Jessica was aware of Robert's eyes on her face, of her sisters clustering around her, of the tension emanating from her mother. Lizzie's green eyes were like emeralds.

Harry held out one hand in a theatrical gesture. "Miss Jessica Beverley," he said, "will you do me the very great honour of accepting my hand in marriage?"

There was a silence. Jessica glanced up as if aware in that moment of being watched from above and saw Miss Trumble at the back of the musicians' gallery. Miss Trumble shook her head, begging Jessica to refuse. Then Lizzie gave Jessica an angry little push in the small of the back and Jessica began to walk slowly forwards. People parted to let her through, Robert, Honoria, Mary Judd among them.

Harry seized Jessica's hand in his own. Her face was very white, he noticed. He had a sudden awful feeling she was about to refuse him. She curtsied and he bent his head over her as if listening to what she was saying. Then he straightened up, holding her hand in a fierce grip. "The lady says yes," he announced.

There was a roar of applause. Jessica looked around her, bewildered. "You did mean yes, did you not?" said Harry in her ear and she nodded dumbly. She had succeeded where Isabella had failed. The musicians began to play a waltz. She stumbled slightly as she moved in Harry's arms. Faces came and went in front of her wide-eyed gaze: Mary Judd, hard and bitter; Honoria with an odd mocking, triumphant gleam in her eyes; her sisters, radiant and happy. And then she looked up at the possessive look in Harry's eyes. She immediately looked away and up towards the musicians' gallery. But Miss Trumble had gone.

Miss Trumble and Barry made their way silently out of Mannerling and round to their carriage. When they reached the gates of Mannerling, Miss Trumble was the first to break the silence as she sat beside Barry, wrapped in a bearskin travelling rug.

"So that is that."

"I suppose so, miss. And yet . . ."

"And yet what?"

"There is still hope."

Miss Trumble looked upwards towards the uncaring stars. "I see none. Do you think the stars influence our destinies, Barry?"

"I think often it is us, miss, who make things the way they are. But have you considered that Mr. Harry might yet, before the wedding day, reveal himself in his true colours? If he lives up to his reputation with women, then there is hope that he might."

"He may, like most of his kind, have settled on a gently bred lady to ornament his home and will seek his pleasures among the Cyprians of London."

"I do not think you really believe that."

There was a short silence and then Miss Trumble said sadly, "Perhaps you are right. I did not like the way he looked at her. God help Jessica Beverley."

Jessica had moved into the supper-room on the arm of Harry Devers. She overheard Miss Turlow saying loudly, "Well, that lot have finally secured the prize." Robert was passing Miss Turlow when she spoke and that fact added to Jessica's misery. Why should she feel so wretched when she had finally secured what they had all only dreamt of?

What she considered her duty to her family came to her rescue and she forced herself to smile at Harry and flirt with him while a nagging headache grew in severity.

Perhaps only Robert was not fooled by Jessica's well-affected happiness. He saw the strain behind her eyes and tried to comfort himself by considering that the girl was getting only what she deserved.

Another of the Beverley sisters was far from happy. Lizzie did not like the way Honoria had dismissed her. She remembered guiltily how much she had confided in Honoria and how Honoria had told her about Harry's failure to secure the hand of Miss Habard. She suddenly wished to escape from the ballroom and collect her thoughts. Murmuring an excuse to her mother, who was next to her at the supper-table, Lizzie not having a partner, she said she wished to rearrange her hair. She made her way down to the ante-room reserved for the ladies' cloaks. The maids, including Betty, were sitting on chairs in the hall, chatting to the footmen, and so the little room was empty. She sat down at the dressing-table in front of the mirror that had been placed there so that the ladies could repair their appearances. She picked up a hairbrush and began to brush her long red hair, which she still wore down. A young lady came in, saw Lizzie, and said, "Are there any pins there? That friend of Harry Devers, Captain Gully, trod on my gown and ripped a flounce."

"There is a bowl of pins here," said Lizzie. "Would you like me to pin your gown for you?"

"If you please. You are very kind. I must introduce myself. I am Margaret Palfrey, and you are the youngest of the Beverleys, are you not?"

Lizzie held out her hand. "Lizzie Beverley. Yes, I am the youngest." She shook Margaret's hand and then took some pins and knelt on the floor and began to neatly pin up the torn flounce.

"Are you very happy about your sister's engagement?"

"Oh, so very happy," mumbled Lizzie through the pins in her mouth.

"Miss Habard, to whom Harry proposed, is my closest friend."

Lizzie finished pinning the flounce and stood up. "There! That should hold. But I did not think Mr. Harry had actually proposed to Miss Habard. The way I heard it, he decided not to because he was enamoured of Jessica."

"I am sure that is what he would like people to believe," said Margaret stiffly.

"But surely that was what happened," protested Lizzie.

"Miss Honoria Sommerville herself told me that was the case."

"I had the story from Miss Habard *and* her parents," said Margaret. "He had asked her parents' permission and received it. As they had been invited to Mannerling that day, it was arranged between the Habards and the Deverses that the proposal should take place there. Harry Devers took Miss Habard–Annabelle–into the rose garden. He proposed in a most offhand way and when she said her parents had chosen a property for them, he said they would live at Mannerling after they were married. Then he grabbed her and mauled her and treated her like the veriest prostitute. She ran away in distress and told her parents she could never marry him."

"No!" said Lizzie, raising her hands to her face.

"Oh, yes, and Miss Habard said it might have been worse had she not hit out at him and then run away. I am heartily sorry for your sister."

"You are jealous!" panted Lizzie, suddenly furious. "I will not listen to another word!"

"Believe what you like," said Margaret scornfully. "It is well known that you Beverley girls would put your own mother on the auction block at Smithfield if it would get your precious Mannerling back."

Lizzie's cheeks flamed. "Be quiet! No more!"

"No? Well, why I should bother putting you wise is beyond me. Have you also heard that it is also well known to everyone but Mr. Sommerville that his sister, Honoria, does not wish him to get married?"

"Go away," said Lizzie miserably. "Oh, please, just go away."

Margaret left with a toss of her curls. Lizzie sat down suddenly and stared blindly at the mirror. Had her own burning ambition to come home to Mannerling at all costs left her open to the plots of Honoria? And was Harry Devers really so bad?

In that moment she thought of Miss Trumble, longing to confide in the governess and hear words of calm good sense. But what else would Miss Trumble say other than that Robert Sommerville was a fine man and that Jessica had made a terrible mistake?

Lizzie looked around the ante-room. It had always been used as a cloakroom when the Beverleys had given balls and parties at Mannerling. She remembered when she was very young, too young to attend one of the grand balls, sneaking down the back stairs through a little door that led to the back of the room and peering round it, watching the ladies in their beautiful gowns leaving their wraps, cloaks, and shawls. She had imagined making her come-out, not in London, but here in Mannerling. Angry tears filled her eyes and she brushed them away. She was too young for Margaret's words about Harry's lechery to make much of a lasting impact on her. Margaret must be jealous, of course she must! That was why she had said all those dreadful things.

She sat there for a long time composing herself, and then made her way up the grand staircase to the ballroom. Supper was over and Jessica was once more partnered by Harry. There was colour in her cheeks and she looked happy. Lizzie let out a little sigh of relief.

Lizzie was not to know that Jessica, under a smiling mask, was feeling bewildered. Harry had not drunk overmuch at supper and he had said charming things about how happy they would be together at Mannerling, how his parents would live elsewhere, and how she would be mistress of the place and be able to make any changes she wished. This was what she and her sisters had dreamt of. The hunt was over, the fox was well and truly caught, so why did she feel so very sad? Why was she conscious all the time of every move that Robert Sommerville made?

Towards the end of the evening, Robert at last came up to her and asked her to partner him in the waltz. No sooner were they on the floor, no sooner did he have his arm round her waist, then he bent his dark head and said, "So at last you have all you want."

"Yes, I thank you," said Jessica in a low voice.

"Perhaps sacrifice makes you happy?"

"There is no sacrifice, sir."

"Then I must be happy, too. For when I found out how my own sister had engineered your abrupt departure from my home, I felt in part responsible for this folly."

"Your sister . . . how?"

"Knowing your ambitions and yet hoping you had grown out of them, I kept the news from you that Harry was not to wed Miss Habard. But my sister cultivated the friendship of young Lizzie, wrote to Mrs. Devers, found that Harry was still free, and told Lizzie. As she expected, the news sent all of you scampering off home."

Jessica was too shocked to protest that her mother had indeed been ill. "But Lizzie told us that Harry did not propose to Miss Habard because he said he was enamoured of me."

Now it was Robert who was shocked. He knew what Mrs. Devers had written to Honoria and in her letter she had said nothing about Harry's turning down Miss Habard because of love for Jessica. Honoria must have embellished her tale with lies to make sure the Beverleys left.

"Such was not the case," he said, his face rigid with distaste. "My sister wanted rid of you, and as I pointed out, she was successful."

Jessica now felt miserable with shame. She remembered their stay at Tarrant Hall, which now seemed in retrospect like a sunny, carefree idyll. "Tell me," she said, "why it was that Harry did not propose to Miss Habard?"

"He did propose, but–how shall I put it delicately–he mauled and pawed her in a way a lady should never be handled, and she took fright."

"You surely have only Miss Habard's word for that?"

"They were in the rose garden in full view of both Mr. and Mrs. Devers and Mr. and Mrs. Habard, who witnessed the end of the romance."

"I have my duty to my family," said Jessica, her voice now barely above a whisper, but he caught what she said just the same.

"I should be furious with you for your clumsy, thoughtless, and hurtful behaviour," he said, "but I pity you for the grim future that lies in front of you."

Jessica's pride came to her rescue. "I consider myself the most fortunate of ladies," she said, and so they waltzed on until the end of the dance in an angry silence.

And yet, had Harry shown the slightest sign of manhandling her that evening or subjecting her to any of the behaviour that had so frightened Miss Habard, she might have begged her mother's help in crying off. But fortunately for Jessica's peace of mind, Harry, who had every intention of trying to get her alone before the end of the ball and "sampling the goods," as he described it to himself, came upon a distraction. Mrs. Devers, despite her haughtiness, was a clever hostess. She knew that no ball or event could be deemed a success if most of the guests left before the end, and so she had hired an Italian diva, Madam Maria Lanni, to entertain the company. Chairs had been arranged in rows in the hall, the orchestra moved out onto the landing, and the diva took up her position in front of them at the top of the grand staircase. In the shuffling and pushing to get seats, Jessica found herself next to Robert. She could not rise to join Harry. Firstly, it would look rude, and secondly, there was a more practical reason. The Devers family had secured seats for themselves in the front row, and there were no empty seats next to them.

Harry's sudden interest was not in the music but in Maria Lanni's magnificent figure. She was a short woman but with a huge, deep bosom, which spilled over the low top of a black velvet gown. She had a full, fleshy mouth, large round eyes, and a thin, straight, and rather long nose. The fact that her voice was quite beautiful did not affect Harry's senses. Perhaps Mannerling itself was the only thing ever in his life that had raised his thoughts above the material and carnal.

Jessica sat beside Robert, listening to that liquid, melting voice singing of lost love. The chairs were jammed close together. His shoulder was pressed against hers. She felt as if her very bones were melting, her breath became rapid, she felt trapped by that touch of his shoulder and by the soaring music in a cage of emotion. As a savage prays to a pagan god, so Jessica prayed to Mannerling to exert its old spell and enchantment. But she was aware only of Robert and the music and the music and Robert until she felt quite faint.

When the concert was finally over, Jessica mumbled something, rose quickly to her feet, and made her escape. She sought out her mother and said shakily that she would like to go home. "There are only two more dances," said Lady Beverley. " 'Twould be rude to leave now, as this is the most important evening in your life. It is not usual for a gentleman to dance with a lady more than twice, but on this special occasion Mr. Harry will want the last dance with you."

Somehow Jessica found she was dreading dancing with Harry. She had thought that escape from Robert's proximity would give her senses relief, but she felt lost and bereft. And when the last dance was announced, Harry was nowhere to be seen, Robert had already asked a pretty young girl, and so Jessica's hand was claimed by the oily vicar, Mr. Stoppard, who had snubbed the Beverleys quite disgracefully since their ruin but was now anxious to ingratiate himself.

Fortunately for Jessica, it was a rowdy country dance and the vicar had little opportunity to speak to her.

The Beverleys said good night to Mr. and Mrs. Devers. Mrs. Devers looked flustered and said she did not know where Harry could have got to, although the poor boy was so delicate and sensitive that perhaps the excitement of the evening had been too much for him.

Maria Lanni was eating a late meal in a corner of the supper-room. The door had been closed and locked to give the diva privacy, but Harry, having found out where she was, took the spare key from the butler's pantry, unlocked the door and slipped inside, and locked it behind him.

He lounged across the room and sat down next to Maria. She continued to eat, ignoring him. "You've got a beautiful voice," said Harry, his eyes fastened greedily on her bosom. She wiped her mouth on the table-cloth and said in a slightly cocknified voice, "So I believe."

Harry gave an inward sigh. He was always bored with the formality of paying compliments.

But the diva drained the wine in her glass, poured another, and said, "How much?"

"How much do I like your singing? Beats the nightingales every time, believe me."

"I mean, how much you pay me for my favours?"

Harry goggled. "You mean . . . I mean . . ."

"I have met your kind before," said Maria. "It always comes to the same thing. So I ask you again . . . how much?"

Harry's palms felt sweaty. She leaned back in her chair and the candle-light fell on the whiteness of her magnificent breasts, revealed by the low-cut gown.

"How much are you asking?" His voice was hoarse.

"You are Mr. Harry Devers, are you not?"

Harry nodded dumbly.

"So the good hostess, Mrs. Devers, is your mother?"

Again Harry nodded.

"Your mama is wearing a fine diamond necklace. Get it for me and bring it to my room."

"Can't do that," said Harry. "I say, I'll buy you one of your own."

"Mama's necklace . . . or good night."

"Damme, there's no one here. I could take you now."

"I have a good voice. One scream from me would be heard not only here but in London. And I would give my story to the newspapers."

"Joke," said Harry feebly. And then his eyes brightened. He knew his mother kept paste replicas of all her jewels and was often reluctant to wear the real gems, preferring to keep them safely in the bank. Tonight the necklace she was wearing was the real thing, but the paste one would be in the jewel-box in her room.

"It's yours," he said eagerly. "What about a kiss?"

"Nothing, my friend, until I have the diamonds around my neck."

"I'll get 'em." Harry rose to his feet. She continued to drink wine, watching him with hard bright eyes as he bowed, turned, and marched to the door.

The last dance was being announced. He forgot about Jessica, his engagement, about everything except Maria's charms. He went quietly up the stairs to his mother's bedroom. To his relief, her lady's-maid was absent. He lit an oil-lamp and began to search feverishly. It seemed to take a long time. He was dimly aware of the sound of carriage wheels in the drive as the guests left and only gave a brief passing thought that he should have said goodbye to them. He found the jewel-box at last at the bottom of a large wardrobe. He dragged it out. It was locked. He searched frantically for the key, and then remembered with a sinking heart that the lady's-maid kept the keys with the others—of the lace-box, tea-box, and things like that—on a chain at her waist. He swore loudly and was about to give up when, as he raised the oil-lamp high for a last look around, he caught the sparkle and shine from something hidden under a gauzy scarf on the toilet-table. He ripped the scarf aside and a slow smile crossed his lips. For there was the paste necklace. His mother must have had it out before the ball, debating whether to wear it or the real one. Without a thought for the poor lady's-maid who would probably be blamed for its disappearance, he snatched it up and stuffed it in his pocket.

Whistling blithely, he made his way out and up the back stairs and so along to Maria's room.

Maria had changed into a loose flowing gown. Her maid was brushing her hair. She saw Harry's reflection in the mirror and said to her maid, "Leave us."

Harry grinned as he went up to her. He barely heard the closing of the door behind him as the maid left. He took out the diamonds and fastened the gleaming strands about her neck.

She smiled and then said, "Come to bed."

And for the first time in his life, Harry Devers met a lust that matched his own. The sun was high in the sky when he left her and went silently to his own room and descended into an exhausted sleep. He had not thought of Jessica once.

Chapter Seven

For, as our different ages move,
'Tis so ordained (would fate but mend it!)
That I shall be past making love
When she begins to comprehend it.

—*Matthew Prior*

Robert Sommerville was fascinated only by the charms of Maria Lanni's voice when he found her still in residence by the following evening. She for her part was content to converse amiably at the dinner table with a gentleman who knew all about opera, although she was cunningly aware the whole time of Harry's hot and jealous eyes fastened on her face.

When the ladies retired to leave the gentlemen to their wine, Mrs. Devers said to Maria, "Will you be staying with us for very long?"

"Does it inconvenience you, ma'am?"

"No," lied Mrs. Devers, who was finding the opera singer's presence not only inconvenient but a great worry as well. She had noticed the way Harry had been staring at the wretched woman. She had suggested to him that he might like to call on Jessica and invite her to come and stay, but Harry had said hurriedly that he would see enough of the girl once they were married–hardly the remark of a lover. "We do plan to go to London in a few days' time," she went on smoothly. "I do not want to send you so hurriedly on your way, but . . ." She pointedly let the sentence trail away.

"Thank you so very much for inviting me to stay until your departure," said Maria, and Mrs. Devers, who had no intention of travelling to London, began to think she would have to go in order to get rid of this dangerous and unwelcome guest.

Robert, on his way to his own room that night along the dimness of the corridor lit only by one oil-lamp, saw Harry's tall figure disappearing into Maria's bedchamber. He thought of Jessica. He tried not to. If Harry was as infatuated with Maria as he appeared to be, there was a hope the engagement could be broken.

He hesitated outside his own room, his hand on the handle of the door. Then, against his will, against every voice that was screaming in his head that he was not behaving like a gentleman, he went along the corridor and listened outside Maria's door.

He heard Harry's voice, loud with anger. "You've already had Mama's diamond necklace; you can't have her tiara as well. Don't you realize the servants will be blamed when it is found they are missing?"

And then came Maria's mocking voice. "I think then I shall take my leave tomorrow and sleep alone tonight."

Harry's voice dropped to a pleading mumble. Then Maria said quite clearly, "No tiara, no favours, my young buck." And then came Harry's voice, aggrieved and petulant, "Oh, all right!"

Robert moved quickly back to his room. He felt grubby for having listened. What had happened to him? He had stooped to reading his sister's private correspondence, and now he was listening at doors. Harry had obviously given the opera singer his mother's diamond necklace, and now he was planning to give her the tiara as well. The minute Mrs. Devers missed them, there would be an outcry. The servants would be accused of theft. Something had to be done. Not so long ago, he would have talked it over with Honoria, but he had had another angry scene with his sister after the ball, and she had left the next morning for Tarrant Hall. He decided to sleep on it.

The following day, Mrs. Devers's maid approached her mistress, tears running down her face. "What is it, Justine?" asked Mrs. Devers. The maid's name was Peggy, but Mrs. Devers always gave her lady's-maids French names in the hope of making them look fashionable. She had employed a succession of lady's-maids, and "Justine" had lasted the longest, that period of employment being now five months.

"Your diamonds have gone," wailed the maid. "I did not like to tell you, but the paste diamond necklace was missing after the ball, but I thought it might have fallen down somewhere; but now the tiara has gone as well!"

And so the butler and housekeeper were summoned, Mr. Devers was told of the theft, and soon the great house was in an uproar. Robert, coming back from a morning's ride, quickly learned that the theft had been discovered. He felt a distaste for the whole sorry business and longed to keep quiet about it. He wondered whether Maria knew the jewels were fake. Just before dinner, he took Justine aside and said quietly, "This is a difficult affair; I regret to tell you that you will probably find your mistress's jewels in the opera singer's bedroom. Reclaim them when she is at dinner, tell your mistress quietly about it, and we can hush up the scandal that way."

And so, had it worked out that way, Maria would have been taken aside and told to leave for London immediately. But before that could happen, Mrs. Devers said at the dinner table, "I know the wretched jewels were only paste, but nonetheless, they were excellent copies and I do not like to lose them. If they are not found soon, then we shall need to tell the authorities."

Maria's eyes widened. "Paste?" she demanded.

"Yes, paste," said Mr. Devers. "My wife's paste diamond

necklace and tiara have gone missing."

Maria got to her feet, her magnificent bosom heaving. Harry tugged at the sleeve of her velvet gown. "Sit down," he hissed, "and keep quiet."

The opera singer rounded on him. "Paste!" she shouted. "You gain my favours and this is how you repay me! Paste!"

"What is this, Harry? What is she talking about?" asked Mrs. Devers.

"Nothing, nothing," said Harry.

Maria sat down slowly. She realized she could hardly tell her hosts how she had come by the jewels, although she had practically already done so. And then the butler, who had been called out of the room, came in and stooped low over Mrs. Devers and whispered something that made that lady's face go rigid with shock and disgust.

Mrs. Devers looked straight at Maria. "I shall tell the servants you will be leaving in the morning, Miss Lanni."

Maria threw Harry a look fit to kill, but said nothing. The meal progressed in grim silence. Then Maria rose to her feet. "I am fatigued," she announced, "and will retire."

Mr. and Mrs. Devers waited until she had gone and the double doors were closed behind her.

"Harry," began Mrs. Devers, "this is the outside of enough. You plague us and threaten us until you not only get permission to wed Jessica Beverley but to get Mannerling as well, and now, shortly after your engagement is announced, you shame this family by stealing my jewels and giving them to a trollop."

Robert got to his feet. "I've had enough of this," he said. "I'm going out for a walk."

"I will come with you," said Harry.

"Sit down!" barked his father.

Harry sat down and stared sulkily at his plate as Robert swiftly left the room. "I knew they were only paste," he said. "I did it for a lark."

"We have gone along with all your disgraceful plans,"

said Mr. Devers. "We have allowed you to sell out, we have allowed you to propose to a girl of no means to speak of and one who has made her ambitions to live here again very blatant, and you have made us promise to move out of this house, and this is how you repay us! But perhaps marriage will save you. We will summon Lady Beverley here tomorrow, you will get a special licence, and you will marry Jessica Beverley in six weeks' time or we will cut off your allowance."

Harry began to bluster. "I'm not such a bad chap. Got to have a bit of fun. I mean, I'm going to settle down and be a staid married man any day now." He thought of the voluptuous charms of Maria. Just give him one more night with her, and surely this aching lust would be assuaged. His mind searched this way and that for a way out.

He sighed. "You have the right of it. You are loving parents and I have treated you damnably. Damme, I love you both. Go ahead and see Lady Beverley. I will go to my regiment tomorrow and make all well with my colonel, for we left on bad terms and I would like him to attend the wedding." He stretched out his hand to his mother. "Forgive me, Mama."

A weak smile fluttered on her lips. "You are such a rogue, Harry."

Mr. Devers, who had been taken aback by his son's first declaration of love for them, began, as he had done in the past, to make excuses for Harry in his mind. The singer had obviously corrupted and seduced his boy. She was an evil woman. The jewels had only been paste. Harry had known that. He brushed aside an uneasy thought that Harry had never been able to tell paste diamonds from the real thing.

"You may go and see your colonel," he said. "But I think you should get that special licence. Children is what you need, a nursery full of children, fine sons. Marriage will settle you."

"You are very good to me," said Harry in a broken voice,

and had the private satisfaction of seeing his parents smile mistily at each other. All Harry wanted to do was to follow Maria to London. He had no intention of going near his colonel.

Robert walked for a long time across country, barely noticing where he was going until he found his footsteps were leading him to Brookfield House. He knew he should forget Jessica. She had behaved disgracefully.

The night was bright with stars and the moonlight sent his shadow moving across the grass in front of him. He stopped at the end of the short drive that led to Brookfield House. And then he saw Jessica walking in the garden. Her hair was down her back and she was wrapped in a warm cloak. Up and down she paced under the moon. He longed to call out to her and tell her of Harry's perfidy, but she would not believe him and he would despise her the more. He turned away.

"Who's there?" he heard her call.

He turned back. "It is I, Robert Sommerville." He opened the gate and went into the garden to join her.

"What brings you here?" asked Jessica. "Have you come to call on us?"

"No, I went out for a long walk and found myself here. I shall not disturb you any longer."

"Stay. We have not really talked much since my visit to your home."

"There is nothing to talk about. You soon will have Harry to talk to."

About what? thought Jessica miserably. But she said, "How are things at Mannerling?"

"There has been some unpleasantness in the family, and so I quit the dinner table and left them to their arguments."

"About me?"

"No, not about you. But I may as well tell you, that you and your mama are to be summoned to Mannerling tomorrow. Mr. and Mrs. Devers have decided that you and Harry should be married by special licence in six weeks' time."

"So soon?" Jessica's voice was a wail of dismay. "That is not enough time to get a wedding gown made."

"I thought you would be delighted. You will be back in Mannerling in no time at all."

"Mannerling." Her voice was a sigh.

"And you will be happy?"

"My sisters will be happy. Where is Harry?"

"At Mannerling. How you must be counting the minutes until you see him again."

Jessica turned her head away. He put a strong hand under her chin and raised her face up to his. Her eyes were wide and dark in the moonlight.

"Are . . . are you going to kiss me?" asked Jessica in a trembling voice.

"No, you are engaged to Harry, and so I will never kiss you again. In fact, I should not be here alone with you. Good night, Miss Jessica." He released her. She stood sadly and watched him walk away, longing to call him back, but unable to think of any reason for doing so.

That night Lizzie could not sleep. She decided to go down to the kitchen and get herself a glass of milk. As she passed Jessica's door she heard the sounds of weeping. She gently opened the door and went in.

"Jessica," whispered Lizzie. "What is wrong? What is the matter?"

"A bad dream, Lizzie," said Jessica. "Go away. I will be all right now."

Lizzie left and went down to the kitchen. She did not think Jessica had experienced a bad dream. Her conviction that Jessica was marrying Harry only to please her family was weighing down on her. She felt if she did not talk about it to someone, she would be plagued with guilt.

Miss Trumble was a light sleeper. She awoke as soon as Lizzie entered the room and, struggling up against the pillows, saw the little form of Lizzie in the dim light from the pierced canister of the night-light beside the bed.

"Why, Lizzie!" she exclaimed. "Are you ill?"

Lizzie nervously approached the bed. "I wanted to talk. I am worried–but if you are tired . . ."

"No, no, come and sit on the bed, child, and tell me what ails you. People of my age do not need much sleep."

Lizzie sat down on the edge of the bed. "It's about Jessica. She's crying. She says she had a bad dream. But I do not believe her."

"And why is that?"

"Oh, I must tell you. I fear I have been badly gulled. When Miss Palfrey told me, I thought it was because she was jealous."

"Who is Miss Palfrey?"

"A young lady I met at the ball."

"And what did she tell you?"

In a halting voice, Lizzie told Miss Trumble everything she had learned, repeating over and over, between each sentence, that it could not be true.

"I think it *is* true," said Miss Trumble when Lizzie had finished. "I wondered why such a woman as Honoria Sommerville sought your company. I would have judged it not to be in her nature. And I am sure you told her all about Mannerling and how you hoped to win the place back. She tricked you and your family into leaving, although," added Miss Trumble, "as far as Harry Devers being a lecher is concerned, I fear that is the case."

"What have I done?" wailed Lizzie.

"My child, you have done nothing. Had Jessica not been so blindly ambitious, nothing you could have told her would have made her cut short her visit to Mr. Sommerville. I think you must be strong and leave things as they are. Only Jessica can break the engagement, and when she is ready to do that, you must tell me and I will do all in my power to support her. She may be miserable now, but not miserable enough to give up Mannerling. And you, too, must give up any thoughts of Mannerling, Lizzie. It is ruining your young life, a life, I believe, you nearly took?"

Lizzie nodded her head.

"You must never do such a thing again, Lizzie. If you feel desperate again, then you must come to me. And we will talk and talk until your obsession with Mannerling leaves you." She leaned forward and put her arms around the girl and hugged her close. Lizzie gave a little sigh and leaned her head against Miss Trumble's thin chest. "But you will go away," said Lizzie, her voice choking on a sob. "Mama was saying only the other day that perhaps we had enough of learning."

"I will stay until you are married, Lizzie."

"I may never marry. I am not beautiful like my sisters."

"When your time comes, you will outshine them. Now go to bed and try not to worry. Jessica must resolve her problems herself."

Miss Trumble could not help noticing the next day how heavy-eyed Jessica looked. The arrival of a footman from Mannerling with a note summoning both Jessica and Lady Beverley to Mannerling "for a family consultation" was met by complacency by Lady Beverley and a sort of stiff-faced acceptance by Jessica.

On arriving at Mannerling, Jessica tried not to feel relieved when she was told that Harry was absent. She hoped the hurried wedding was to be put off. But Mr. and Mrs. Devers told Lady Beverley that their son was anxious for an early wedding and they would like to set the date for six weeks' time.

Jessica hoped her mother would protest, but all Lady Beverley did was smile indulgently and murmur something about the impetuosity of youth.

"There will not be time to have a wedding gown made," said Jessica.

"I know a very good woman in Hedgefield," said Mrs. Devers, who never had any of her gowns made outside London.

Lady Beverley gave a trilling laugh, the sort of laugh taught to ladies by singing teachers, starting at the top note and rippling down the scale. "We cannot possibly have a Beverley going to the altar in a country gown. Isabella left her wedding gown behind. That will do very well, for she and Jessica are of a size."

Mr. Devers looked anxiously at Jessica. She looked sad and wan. He felt a stab of pity for her.

"Perhaps Miss Jessica does not relish the idea of being married in her elder sister's cast-off," he said.

"No, it is all right," said Jessica wearily. "I do not mind, I assure you."

The door opened and Robert Sommerville came in. His clever, handsome face was sombre as he looked at his aunt and uncle and then at the visitors. "I beg your pardon," he said, giving a low bow.

"Pray join us," said Mrs. Devers graciously. "We are about to have tea."

Mr. Devers noticed that a pink colour was now staining Jessica's face. Robert sat down. He did not look at Jessica and she did not look at him, but the air between them seemed to crackle with tension.

Lady Beverley began to talk about the countryside, how various of the Mannerling tenants were faring–she had not visited any of them but had picked up gossip about people on the estate from Miss Turlow, whom she had met in the mercer's the week before–quite in her old manner of mistress of Mannerling. Mrs. Devers said crossly that she herself never visited the tenants because that was the job of the factor.

"But my dear Mrs. Devers, one always feels it is one's duty." Lady Beverley gave her hostess a complacent smile, and in that moment Mrs. Devers wished her wayward son had settled for an heiress, a meek and dutiful girl, and not one burdened with a family whose one ambition was to regain the house and lands.

With a slight edge in her voice, she looked at Jessica and said sweetly, "It is so pleasant to witness a love match in this mercenary age. I have paid no attention to the gossip that the Beverleys only wish to reclaim Mannerling. People are so unkind, do you not think? More tea, Jessica?"

"No, I thank you." Jessica's voice was so low, it was barely above a whisper.

"The day is fine and not too cold," said Robert suddenly. "Perhaps Miss Jessica would care to walk in the gardens with me and leave you all to discuss guest lists and wedding arrangements."

"I don't think . . ." began Mr. Devers uneasily, but Mrs. Devers inclined her head and said it was a good idea.

When they were out of doors, Jessica said, "Do not begin to question me about how myself and Mama could sit there and let Mrs. Devers talk about our sole ambition being to reclaim Mannerling without protesting or trying to defend ourselves."

"Perhaps because you cannot protest. But enough of that. Are you really prepared to go through with this?"

"I must."

"Then I must leave the subject and leave Mannerling."

Her eyes flew to his face. "You will not stay for the wedding?"

"No, I have much to do. I must see the lawyers and turn Tarrant Hall over to my sister."

"Why? It seemed a most pleasant place."

"Honoria dared to interfere in my life because she wishes to remain mistress of Tarrant Hall. I will not brook such behaviour. I shall buy myself another property."

"That seems an extreme measure."

"Sometimes one must be ruthless to get what one wants. False duty to one's family is a mistake. If one does the right thing—how can I explain?—if one does what is best for oneself, *morally* best, then things will work out. This is not a case of doing what is selfishly best."

"Do you mean that by doing my duty to my family by marrying Harry I am making a mistake?"

They had walked a little way from the house. He took her shoulders and swung her around. "There is the reason for your sacrifice. Look at it! It is a house, nothing more."

And Jessica looked. A cloud had crossed the sun and the house looked dark and somehow sad. She could feel the old spell of Mannerling surging about her. By marrying Harry she could regain what she had lost, all the sunny days of ease and comfort.

She owed it to her family, and she owed it to Mannerling. Robert let his hands drop to his side. What would happen if he burnt the place down? he wondered wildly. Would the Beverleys mourn and then continue, one after the other, to make disastrous marriages in the hope of finding a husband with enough wealth to rebuild the place? The new term at Oxford would soon begin. Back to the cloistered life, away from the lovely Jessica and her obsession, away from Honoria and her interference in his affairs.

He gave a little sigh and then said, "It grows cold. Let us return."

Jessica was sharply aware of his renewed disappointment in her. As they walked in silence towards the house, she realized that Mannerling had suddenly lost its spell for her again, and she was only aware of this tall, handsome man at her side, a man who could have been hers. But there was only Harry now to look forward to. Perhaps something would happen to him? Perhaps *he* would change his mind, rejoin his regiment, cry off.

* * *

When Lady Beverley and Jessica had left, Mr. Devers turned to his wife and said, "I do think it is time Robert ended his visit."

"Why?"

"Because I think he is enamoured of Jessica Beverley and I think the girl is not indifferent to him."

Mrs. Devers groaned. "I think this is too much. I think we should persuade Harry to end the engagement."

"Only Jessica can do that. The Beverleys could sue him for breach of promise. He proposed to her in the most public way possible, and an announcement has been sent to the newspapers."

Mrs. Devers shivered. "I shall be glad to leave here. This place has changed Harry. He was always such a sweet boy." And so once again she conveniently forgot all the scandals and trouble Harry had caused them before they even came to Mannerling.

Two weeks passed and there was no news of Harry. In despair, Mr. Devers sent an express to Harry's colonel, ordering his son's return. The colonel's reply was prompt and also by express. He had seen nothing, nor had he heard anything, of Harry Devers.

Harry was in London. He had gone through a considerable amount of money to satisfy his mistress, Maria Lanni. He had bought her jewels, he had bought her a house, and in order to do so, he had sold several properties in his name. Although such a sale demanded his father's signature as well, Harry did not trouble himself with such trifles. He forged his father's signature. He had forgotten almost completely about Jessica, being perpetually sunk in a sort of red lust. He was coming to the end of his assets. He had tried to raise money at the tables, but he was an unlucky gambler. Soon he was in serious debt. But the end of his passionate affair with Maria came not because he had run out of money, but because, visiting her in her dressing-room after a rehearsal and finding her door locked, he had kicked the flimsy door open to find Maria naked and locked in the arms of the tenor.

She did not cry out in horror or look in the least ashamed. She dismissed the tenor and put on her clothes and then rounded on him, saying she was sick of him. She described the sickening brutality of his love-making in coarse and crude terms. Mad with rage, he tried to strangle her, but before he could get his hands around her throat, she screamed for help and Harry found himself thrown out of the opera house and into the kennel by burly stage-hands.

He now hated her as much as he had loved her. He still had a key to her house. He went there and took all the jewels he had given her and sold them. Once more Mannerling called to him with its cool beautiful rooms and green lawns. But before leaving London he tried to recoup some of the money he had lost at the tables and succeeded only in losing all the money from the sale of the jewels. He obtained a special licence on the road home and, once at Mannerling, listened indifferently to his parents' complaints, saying he had been doing business in London. The wedding could take place in a fortnight's time, so what was all the fuss about?

Mr. Devers said, "You had best call on your fiancée. You are in serious danger of losing the girl to your cousin Robert."

Harry's eyes narrowed with jealousy. "I'll go there right away. You should have sent Robert packing."

"Fortunately, he sent himself. He is now back in Oxford. But you will get a cool reception. I would not be surprised if she cries off."

Lizzie watched Harry riding towards Brookfield House and wondered why her prayers had not been answered. She had prayed so hard that he would never return. It was all so awful. Jessica was to be married in the local church in a second-hand wedding gown by the horrible Mr. Stoppard, and despite Miss Trumble's kind words, Lizzie still felt it was all her fault. She ran quickly down to the kitchen and peered around the door. It was empty. The cook was out in the garden, talking to Barry. She took a sack of flour from the larder and, hurriedly standing on a chair, she balanced the sack over the half-opened front door. Then she retreated to the shadowy back of the small hall and waited, hoping no one else had witnessed Harry's arrival. She heard the creak of saddle leather as he dismounted and then his voice calling, "Anybody home?"

"Walk in!" called Lizzie.

And Harry did and received the full contents of the bag of flour all over him. As he cursed and coughed and spluttered, Lizzie ran swiftly upstairs.

Lady Beverley heard the commotion and came out of the parlour. She stopped short at the sight of Harry, covered in flour and stamping with rage.

She was so glad to see him, for she had feared the wedding would have to be cancelled, that she ignored the dreadful coarseness of his oaths and called on the servants to lead him in and brush him down. Jessica and her sisters came into the parlour and listened amazed as a still-irate Harry accused every one of them of having played a shabby trick on him.

Harry would have gone on complaining and accusing had he not been stopped short by the weary look on Jessica's face. He gave a sudden smile. "I am a bear to rant so. There now. All is forgiven and forgotten." He turned to Jessica. "I must excuse my long absence. I had business in London, but I obtained the special licence and all is set for the wedding."

Jessica did not look at him but nervously smoothed a cambric handkerchief out on her lap. "Come, girls," said Lady Beverley. "No, not you, Jessica. Mr. Harry, you may have ten minutes to talk to Jessica alone. Lizzie! Come along. Why are you sitting there?"

"All set for the wedding?" asked Harry as soon as they were alone, thinking that Jessica did not look at all as beautiful as he had remembered her to be. Her skin was pale and her eyes were heavy, and her shoulders hunched as if to ward off a blow.

"Yes, thank you."

She stood up and rested one hand on the wood of the mantelpiece. He came up behind her and turned her round. "You are angry with me for staying away so long," he said, taking her in his arms. She turned her head away. "What about a kiss for poor Harry?"

"We are not yet married."

"Don't be missish. We soon will be." He seized her and forced his mouth down on hers. She struggled in his arms and he grew angry. His tongue forced its way between her lips, coarse and rough like the tongue of an animal.

He felt a sharp tug at his coat-tails and a shrill voice cried, "Stop that!"

He released Jessica abruptly and swung round. Lizzie was glaring up at him, her emerald eyes blazing. "She don't like it."

"Get out of here, you saucy miss!" raged Harry. He raised his hand to slap her, but Jessica caught his arm and said, "You had better go."

"I think this marriage might be a mistake." His eyes were blazing.

"Perhaps it is," said Jessica quietly.

His anger left him. "Now, there, we have had our first quarrel, sweeting. I'll be off, but I'll send the carriage for you tomorrow. Mama is dying to see you."

Jessica curtsied low.

Harry turned on his heel and left the room.

Jessica sat down suddenly and Lizzie knelt at her feet and took her cold hands in her own. "You put the bag of flour on the door, did you not?" asked Jessica.

Lizzie nodded. And then she said, "Oh, Jessica, you must

not marry such a man. I will never forgive myself if you do. Mannerling is not worth it."

Jessica looked at her, amazed.

"But, Lizzie, I am doing it for you, for the others!"

"You must not."

"But think of the scandal if I cry off! Mama will go into a decline."

Lizzie's face was hard. "Mama has gone into a decline before and got over it. Listen, I must tell you something." She related how Honoria had tricked her.

"I know all that," said Jessica. "Robert . . . Mr. Sommerville . . . told me."

"And you do not hate me?"

"Lizzie, it was my own ambition and folly that got me in this mess. Nothing is your fault. But how can I cancel the wedding? People have sent gifts."

"Not many gifts, Jessica, and not many people. It was to be a quiet wedding. And in a hand-me-down wedding dress of Isabella's, too. And Mama had a letter from Isabella only this morning. She is about to go into labour and cannot risk the journey. Please, please, speak to Miss Trumble. She will think of something."

"How she will despise me!"

"She will despise you the more if you go through with it. Come with me now."

But at that moment Lady Beverley came into the room, exclaiming in surprise that Harry had left. "Such a fine man, Jessica. You are the luckiest of girls."

Jessica opened her mouth to say she could not go through with the wedding but then suddenly felt she could not bear the scene that would result from such a statement. Better to speak to Miss Trumble first.

It was evening before Jessica could get Miss Trumble to herself. The governess listened quietly and without surprise to

Jessica's story of how she had decided she could not go through with the wedding.

"Then you must go to him and tell him quietly that you have made a mistake."

"I am frightened of him. He is sending the carriage for me tomorrow."

"Then I will go with you. Do not say anything to Lady Beverley. I will simply get in the carriage with you. Besides, you may not have to go through the ordeal of telling him. We will speak to Mr. and Mrs. Devers first."

"It will cause such a scandal," said Jessica.

"I do not think so. I think people will realize that at last the Beverleys have come to their senses."

At that moment Robert Sommerville was driving back towards Mannerling, at times cursing himself for being a fool. Such a visit could only bring pain. He would find the whole place in a bustle of wedding preparations, a happy Jessica, and he would feel bitter and sad.

He had more or less resolved never to see Mannerling or Jessica again, but he had received a letter from his sister, Honoria. In it she had said that as soon as Jessica Beverley was wed, he would come to his senses and give up this mad idea of buying a separate property. It was a wicked waste of money, and a cruel thing to do to his own sister. All he had to do was to realize his folly. Had they not been comfortable before? It was those wretched Beverleys who had spoiled everything. And how he could ever have formed a tendre for such as Jessica Beverley, who was nothing more than a mercenary jade, was beyond her.

And Robert, who had also wondered why he had been so smitten and had in his heart damned Jessica as mercenary, found he bitterly resented any criticism of her. There was a dim little hope in his mind that she might decide not to go through with it. Surely the estimable Miss Trumble would not let her. But as he approached Mannerling and saw the great building lying there under a lowering sky, he thought that there lay his rival, not Harry.

And he wished he had not come.

Chapter Eight

O! beware, my lord, of jealousy;
It is the green-eyed monster which doth mock
The meat it feeds on.

—WILLIAM SHAKESPEARE

Lady Beverley protested most strongly when she caught Miss Trumble on the point of departure for Mannerling the following day. "If anyone is to accompany Jessica, it should be me," she complained.

To her surprise, Jessica paid no attention to her and neither did the governess. They both climbed into the carriage and Jessica called to the coachman to drive on.

Miss Trumble pressed Jessica's hand. "Now, you must not look so pale and worried. We shall speak to Mr. and Mrs. Devers. I will speak to them privately first. It will be short, sharp, and nasty, but then you will be able to return, a free woman again, and take up your life."

But both received a shock when the butler informed them that Mr. Harry was abovestairs in the drawing-room and that Mr. and Mrs. Devers had gone to visit friends on the other side of Hedgefield. "Did not Mr. Harry say we were expected?" demanded Miss Trumble.

"No, miss, he said nothing about it."

"You must not be alone with him," murmured Miss Trumble as they went up the stairs together. Jessica nervously squeezed her hand by way of reply.

Harry glared when he saw the slim, erect figure of the governess. He had carefully planned it so that he would be alone with Jessica. "I do not entertain servants," he said with all his parents' haughtiness.

"Then you must bear with my company until Jessica has said to you what she came here to say," said Miss Trumble. And all in that moment, Harry knew he was going to be jilted. He masked the burning rage he felt.

"Pray be seated."

Jessica and Miss Trumble sat side by side on a sofa.

"Courage. Go ahead, Jessica," said Miss Trumble.

Harry stood in front of the fireplace, looking as bland and friendly as he could.

"I cannot marry you," said Jessica. "I am so very sorry. I fear we should not suit."

He gave a merry laugh. "You must not look so frightened, my dear. Bless me, what a weight off my mind, for I had just come to the same conclusion myself."

Unfortunately, sheer relief restored to Jessica all the beauty that had so recently been faded with worry and misery. He felt a surge of lust added to the black rage in his heart.

"Oh, then we can all be comfortable," said Jessica. "I was so very frightened of coming here and telling you. But what will your parents think of me?"

"In truth, and I do not want to hurt your feelings, they'll be deuced relieved. Always wanted me to marry an heiress. Miss Trumble, you will appreciate that I would like a few words in private with Miss Jessica. We have to discuss the best way to break it to Mama and Papa. As I say, they will be relieved, but they will be irritated as well because of all the letters of apology they will have to send out. Only a few moments, Miss Trumble. If you can be so good as to wait in the little morning-room downstairs? Jessica will join you shortly."

"I shall only be a short time," said Jessica, still happy with relief.

Thus appealed to by both, Miss Trumble felt she could hardly refuse.

"Come along," said Harry, as soon as they were alone. "I want to show you where I practise my fencing. I am a good swordsman." He held open the door of the drawing-room at the opposite end to the one through which Miss Trumble had just left. Glad to have been let off so lightly and anxious to please him, Jessica walked through the door, along a corridor and into a long room where she and her sisters had played games on wet days. No sooner was she inside than, to her dismay, Harry locked the door behind them and pocketed the key.

"Now we shall not be disturbed, my sweeting," he said.

"Miss Trumble is waiting," said Jessica, now becoming frightened. "What is it you want to discuss? We will all help with the letters of apology. We will . . ." Her voice died away, for Harry had picked up a fencing foil, flipped the button off the end, and was pointing the sword towards her.

"Now we will have some fun," he said, advancing on her. "Who are you, you greedy little bitch, to turn down such as me? Dreaming of your precious Robert? Did you know he was here, at Mannerling? But he cannot come to your aid, for I sent him off to see a sick tenant to keep him out of the way. Off with your clothes, and let me see the goods before I have 'em."

"You will have to kill me," said Jessica.

"Oh, no, that would be such a waste. Very well, I shall take what I want."

She opened her mouth to scream, but he leaped towards her and clamped one hand over her mouth while the other tore at her gown.

Miss Trumble waited uneasily in the morning-room and then nervously rose to her feet and hurried back upstairs to the drawing-room. When she found the door locked, she rattled the handle fiercely, and then turned and called for the servants.

Robert, returning, heard her shout and ran up the stairs.

He had ridden only a little way away from Mannerling when the thought had struck him that Harry must be scheming to get Jessica alone. He had been amazed to see Mr. and Mrs. Devers driving off. He was sure Harry had thought up a story to get him out of the way and he had the uncharitable thought that Jessica deserved everything that might be happening to her, although Robert, to do him justice, had not once thought of rape.

"The door's locked," cried Miss Trumble, "and Jessica is alone with Harry."

Robert turned to the butler and said, "Fetch the spare key."

"I cannot, I dare not," said the butler. "Mr. Harry said he was not to be disturbed for any reason, and whoever did so would lose their employ."

"Fool," snarled Robert and drove his riding-boot hard against the lock of the door. But the doors were well made and he had to kick out savagely several times before the double doors splintered open.

The drawing-room was empty. "The far door," he said, running towards it. He pulled it open, and just as he did so, he heard Jessica scream.

Terror had lent Jessica a strength she did not know she possessed. She kicked furiously at Harry, glad that she was wearing serviceable half-boots rather than the usual light slippers she wore in the summer. He winced but kept that hand clamped over her mouth. Summoning all her courage, she pulled back a little and bit down on that hand as hard as she could.

"Vixen!" shouted Harry as Jessica, finding her mouth free at last, screamed for all she was worth. He slapped her hard across the face and she fell, sprawling on the polished wooden floor.

"Open up!" came a shout. Robert's voice.

Jessica stumbled to her feet. "You will hang," she said.

"When did a man ever hang for pleasuring a wench?" he jeered. "The door is locked."

He was about to approach her again when he heard heavy blows on the locked door. Some dim thought that he was well and truly in disgrace and may as well be rewarded for it made him ignore the savage onslaught on the door and grab hold of Jessica and bear her down onto the floor. She twisted and writhed and screamed.

At that moment the door burst open, hanging crazily on broken hinges. Harry leaped to his feet and backed away as Miss Trumble helped Jessica up, crying in dismay at the sight of the girl's bare breasts spilling out of her ripped gown.

Robert advanced on Harry, his fists clenched. Harry seized up his sword again and flipped another one to Robert. "Try to defend yourself, milksop of a professor," he jeered.

Miss Trumble tried to lead Jessica from the room, but she said, "Stay. If he kills Robert, then I will kill him–somehow, someway I will kill him."

The triumphant anger in Harry's face faded as he realized this professor was playing with him, was the better swordsman by far. He began to lash out wildly until Robert, who had knocked the protective button off his own foil, feinted, went under Harry's guard, and pinked him in the shoulder. More feints and more parries, and Robert drove Harry towards the wall and then flicked his sword out of his hand.

"You cannot kill me," panted Harry. "You would need to flee the country and never see your dear Jessica again."

Robert, his eyes blazing, stabbed the point of his sword straight into Harry's shoulder. "There!" he said. "That might disable you for a while."

Harry clutched at his bleeding shoulder, his face white. "You've killed me," he whispered through blanched lips, and then he fell in a dead faint on the floor.

Robert swung round and looked in contempt at the servants clustered in the doorway. "Go about your duties. Mr. and Mrs. Devers shall hear on their return how you were prepared to stand by and let a young lady be nearly raped. Off with you! You disgust me!"

"Come, Jessica," said Miss Trumble gently. "It is all over here. Let us go home. I shall make you a soothing posset and you shall go to bed."

"Do as she says," said Robert wearily. "I had best get a physician to attend to this churl. I have no wish to hang because of the death of such a whoreson."

Jessica allowed herself to be led away. It was not at all like romances, she thought in a dazed and muddled way. Robert should have taken her in his arms, not just stood there, looking tired and disgusted with the whole sorry affair.

"I do not know that I will ever forgive myself," mourned Miss Trumble on the way home. "What was I about, to believe he meant you no harm? But even in my wildest dreams I did not for a moment think he would dare to go so far in a house full of servants, and with me waiting downstairs."

"He's mad," said Jessica with a shiver.

"You are safe and free of him. It will take you some time to recover," said Miss Trumble, pulling the shawls she had collected from Mannerling to cover Jessica's ripped gown closer about her.

Lady Beverley was not much help to Jessica, for she wept and screamed and then went into strong hysterics when she heard what had happened and was only stopped when Miss Trumble slapped her smartly across the face. Jessica's sisters listened in stunned silence to Miss Trumble's story.

"I will go and sit by the side of Jessica's bed," said Miss Trumble, "so that I can be there when she awakes."

When she left the room, there was a long silence. Then Lizzie said, "I am glad she is safe. I am glad it is all over. Not only is Harry Devers mad, but we have all been driven crazy by Mannerling."

"Leave me," said Lady Beverley faintly. "No, not you, Rachel and Abigail. Stay with me. The rest of you go away."

When she was alone with the twins, Lady Beverley said, "I find it all very hard to believe."

Rachel said, "But we saw her. You saw how he had ripped Jessica's gown."

"You do not understand the gentlemen, my dears. Look at it this way. Miss Trumble–who, I may add, takes too much upon herself–said that they had both gone to Mannerling to tell Mr. Harry that the wedding was off. Mr. Harry, I admit, is a man of very strong passions. He was madly in love with Jessica, and yet she tells him two weeks before the wedding that she does not want to marry him. His passions were understandably inflamed."

Rachel looked at her mother, round-eyed. "You mean you would condone such behaviour? Do you mean that Jessica being coarsely assaulted is to be excused?"

"But she was not harmed. And now Mannerling is lost to us. I had hoped to give you both a Season in London, but I do not have the funds. Perhaps had Jessica married Mr. Harry, then we could have found the means." And so she talked on and on while the twins listened until Rachel and Abigail, still in the old grip of that obsession for Mannerling, began, too, to find excuses for Harry in their minds. Perhaps Jessica had been too bold, led him on. Only look how intimate her behaviour with Robert Sommerville had been when they had all stayed at Tarrant Hall.

In the following days and weeks, had Jessica talked of her frightening experience, they would have realized that there was no way to rationalize Harry's behaviour. But Jessica did not talk to anyone but Miss Trumble.

Harry Devers, his arm in a sling, faced his parents. He had been allowed out of bed for the first time and was sitting wrapped in a gaudy banyan. "I tell you," he said, "that Jessica was a bold minx. Fact is, I decided I did not want to marry her. She tore her own gown and began to scream for help as a way of forcing me into marriage."

His father looked at him with cold eyes. "In that case, why did she not force you into marriage?"

"Probably became ashamed of her own wanton behaviour," said Harry sulkily.

"We have Robert's description of what happened, and then there are the servants, whom you threatened with dismissal. The story will have reached London by now. I suggest we buy you a commission in a good regiment and you will take yourself away from Mannerling. My man of business in the City has sent me some interesting documents. You sold all your property. In order to do so, you needed my signature, and so you forged it. So you either rejoin the army or I will disinherit you. Selling that property was the biggest crime you have ever committed." And thus Mr. Devers proved himself to be a true Englishman. There was always an excuse for rape, but for wantonly stealing and losing money, none at all.

In vain did Harry try to plead with his parents. He cajoled, he begged. He saw his mother was weakening, but his father remained adamant.

And so, all too soon, Harry found himself in the family travelling-carriage, bowling down the long drive away from Mannerling. His eyes were filled with angry tears. He blamed the Beverleys for everything that had befallen him. One day, he would return to Mannerling, and one day, he would get his revenge on the Beverleys.

It was early in December when a sharp frost set in and Barry was busy chopping kindling, the sound of his axe ringing out across the frosty air. When Miss Trumble came up to him, he did not recognize her at first, for she was wrapped up in so many shawls and wore a bonnet like a coal-scuttle on her head.

"Good morning, Barry," said Miss Trumble, her breath coming out like steam in the sharp air. "Chilblain time is here again."

"It do be so, miss. And how goes Miss Jessica?"

"Not very well, I am afraid."

"Stands to reason, miss. Mortal fright she did have. We wished Mr. Harry would behave badly to bring her to her senses, but we never thought he would go so far."

"I think he is deranged, and I hope a cannon-ball gets him, may God forgive me. But I think Jessica has recovered from her ordeal. The only problem is that she is grieving over what she has lost."

"Not that house again!"

"No, not Mannerling. I do believe Robert Sommerville is the problem. I think she realized too late that she is in love with him. He never comes to Mannerling, and he certainly does not call here."

"Perhaps he no longer cares for her, miss. Perhaps he has taken her in dislike. I am fond of Miss Jessica, and yet I can understand if Mr. Sommerville had a kind of contempt for her because she was prepared, apparently, to go to any lengths to secure Mannerling."

"I think you have the right of it. And yet if he could see her now! She never thinks of Mannerling. I am sure she thinks only of him. She does not discuss him with me or talks about her feelings, but she keeps finding excuses to talk about the visit to Tarrant Hall and she often wonders if he is still there or if he found another property, things like that."

"I would like to do something," said Barry, "but reckon there's not much can be done."

"I have been thinking of that," said Miss Trumble. "What if we were to travel to Tarrant Hall? If he is no longer there, his sister can hardly refuse to give us his direction. The university term has just ended."

"But how can we leave here? Lady Beverley would certainly not allow us to take the carriage."

"I can hire a post-chaise in Hedgefield."

"But how could we get away together? It would look most odd."

"I have had no leave. I can beg some time off to visit my relatives. I shall leave first. You will drive me into Hedgefield and I will put up at the Green Man. Then you yourself must find a reason to leave. Something that would appeal to the mercenary side of Lady Beverley's nature. You could invent a relative who worked on some estate who needs to see you for the wedding of his daughter. Say that this relative can supply you with a goodly quantity of game for the larder. I think, under those circumstances, we would be allowed to leave."

"Post-chaise costs a mort," said Barry reflectively.

"I have the money," said Miss Trumble, and then added quickly, "I was very thrifty in my previous employ and saved a tidy sum."

"And where were you employed previous, miss?"

"Then that's settled," said the governess, cheerfully ignoring the question. "I will start right away and see if I can persuade Lady Beverley to let me leave."

As Barry helped Miss Trumble and her belongings into the small family carriage a week later, only Lizzie and Jessica were sad to see her go. The others blamed her for working on Jessica to break off the engagement with Harry. Longing for her old home had quite turned Lady Beverley's brain, and the others were too innocent and virginal to realize the full extent of Jessica's ordeal.

"You will return?" demanded Lizzie, catching hold of Miss Trumble's sleeve. "You promised."

"And I never break a promise," said Miss Trumble. "Be good, my girls, and do not neglect your studies in my absence."

As the carriage drove off under a grey sky, Lady Beverley sniffed. "My girls, indeed. I sometimes think I should get rid of that governess. She is a touch too high and mighty for a mere servant."

"But she does so much above and beyond her duties,"

pointed out Jessica. "No one can cure your headaches like Miss Trumble. And look how good she was with Lizzie's earache. We did not even have to call in the physician and so saved ourselves a deal of expense."

"True," admitted Lady Beverley. "But I shall remind her most strongly of her position in this household on her return."

Three days later, Barry left as well, Lady Beverley having at last allowed him to go, the promise of a supply of free game being too much to turn down. Barry wondered, as he walked along the road to Hedgefield to join Miss Trumble at the Green Man, where a mere governess got all the money to travel by post-chaise, and she would need money as well to buy game on the road home. There certainly was a mystery about Miss Trumble.

Chapter Nine

So, if I dream I have you, I have you.
For, all our joys are but fantastical.

—JOHN DONNE

Robert Sommerville was back at Tarrant Hall in a black and gloomy mood. He could not understand why his brain could not control his emotions. All logic screamed at him that Jessica Beverley was not worth a single thought, and yet it seemed to him that there was not a moment in the day when he did not ache for her. He had not even looked at other properties. He had no interest in anything. He felt as grey and overcast as if the winter weather had entered his very soul.

Honoria, who had welcomed him home with every comfort she could think of, was confident at first that he would "come to his senses," but as dreary day followed dreary day during which Robert barely spoke to her, Honoria began to lose confidence in herself for possibly the first time in her life. She began to wonder whether, if she had encouraged Robert in his courtship of Jessica, life would not have been better for her. And surely it could not be worse than it was at present! When, one week after his arrival, Robert came down to breakfast unshaven and in his dressing-gown, and did not shave or get dressed for the rest of that day, she began to despair.

"Robert," she ventured almost timidly at dinner that evening as he slumped in his dining chair, "you appeared to enjoy the company of the Beverleys. Would it not raise your spirits to invite them back?"

She then winced as her brother suddenly smashed his fist down on the dining-table. "Do not mention the name Beverley in this house again!" he roared. And, as if suddenly wearied by his burst of rage, he said in a milder voice that was more terrifying to his sister than any of his shouting, "We do not deal very well now, Honoria. I am too bored and fatigued with life to go searching for a new property. Perhaps you should go on an extended visit to Aunt Matilda in Bath. I believe she is looking for a companion."

"I am happy here," said Honoria miserably. But her brother was striding out of the room and did not hear her words.

"Now, Barry," cautioned Miss Trumble as they saw the tall chimneys of Tarrant Hall rising above the trees, "if Miss Honoria Sommerville is there, we cannot count on a warm welcome. We are servants in her eyes, so we must not state our business if Mr. Robert is not in residence, but find out his direction. He may have decided to stay in Oxford over the Christmas period. It is so difficult being a servant, is it not?"

"Difficult for you, miss, or so it do seem. But for me, I have a comfortable enough billet at Brookfield House and enough to eat. A man cannot ask for more. But now, Miss Trumble, what about you? We stayed at the best posting-houses and you were very much the great lady. It almost seems to me that you are but lately descended to the servant class."

"Flatterer," said Miss Trumble. "Perhaps I should have been an actress, were it not such a disreputable profession. No more, Barry. We are nearly there."

Miss Trumble tried to keep up a brave front as Barry helped her down from the post-chaise. She paid the driver and then waited while Barry performed a tattoo on the brass door-knocker. Miss Trumble was suddenly assailed with doubts. Should Robert Sommerville be at home, then how should she introduce the real reason for her call? Governesses, no matter how genteel, were not welcome as visitors. Why had she been so silly as to have dismissed the post-chaise and driver? What could she say? How could she put it? "Er, Mr. Sommerville, you should reconsider Jessica. I know she preferred a house to you, but she has been forced to change her mind about that matter because, as you know, Harry Devers nearly raped her. I am sure she loves you."

To which he might be justified in replying, "Miss Jessica has proved herself mercenary once and is now doing so again. I am a rich man of estates and property and she has no wealth worth speaking of. You are impertinent to come to my home to speak about this. I shall write to Lady Beverley and suggest that in future she keep a better rein on her staff."

Of course he would not be so brutal as that, so ran Miss Trumble's worried thoughts as the butler answered the door, inclined his head, took her card with the tips of his white-gloved fingers, dropped it on a silver tray as if shaking loose a dead insect, and then marched up the stairs.

He had not asked her to step inside, but Miss Trumble had no intention of shivering on the step. She boldly stepped into the hall and sat down primly on a high-backed chair while Barry stood deferentially at her side, trying to look more like a footman and less like the outdoor servant that he was.

The butler came down the stairs and intoned, "Miss Sommerville will be pleased to receive you, ma'am. Be so good as to step this way."

"Stay here, Barry," murmured Miss Trumble. She felt more nervous than ever as she followed the butler up to the drawing-room. Honoria Sommerville could hardly be expected to give a warm welcome to anyone from the Beverley household, least of all a mere servant.

But to her amazement, Honoria advanced to meet her, taffeta skirts rustling, hands outstretched in welcome. "My dear Miss Trumble, what a pleasant surprise! But you should have written in advance so that a room could be prepared for you. Why are you alone? Come and sit by the fire. The day is unpleasantly cold, is it not?"

Bewildered, Miss Trumble allowed herself to be pressed into a comfortable chair. "You are most kind. I am alone. I actually came to see Mr. Sommerville."

"And so you shall. I shall be honoured if you would join us for dinner. How goes the family?"

"The Beverleys are all well, I thank you." Miss Trumble decided that Honoria was being pleasant to her in order to find some way of using her, or tricking her. Then her heart sank as she thought she had hit on the real answer to this odd welcome. Honoria was confident that her brother wanted nothing more to do with the Beverleys. He was still in residence at Tarrant Hall, and that showed he had surely given up the idea of a separate establishment. Honoria was delighted to show this emissary from the Beverleys that they could give up all hopes of a match between her brother and Jessica.

By unspoken consent, they began to talk of politics, plays, and poetry. Honoria ordered tea for them and they passed a pleasant two hours. Barry had been given a room in the servants' quarters, but, after tea, Miss Trumble was shown to one of the guest apartments and Honoria sent her lady's-maid to attend to Miss Trumble's comfort.

When the dinner gong sounded, Miss Trumble went down to the dining-room, following the footman who had been sent to light her way with a branch of candles.

Robert Sommerville rose to his feet, his eyes wary and guarded. "How pleasant to see you, Miss Trumble," he said. He asked her questions about her journey and then, as his sister had done earlier, he began to talk of everything except the Beverley family. Poor Miss Trumble knew that soon she would have to ask if she could speak to him in private but did not quite know how to go about it. At last, she decided to enjoy her meal as best she could and seek him out in the morning. But when dinner was over and Honoria rose to lead Miss Trumble from the dining-room, Robert said quietly, "Leave our guest with me, Honoria."

Honoria hesitated for a moment as if longing to stay and hear what it was Miss Trumble had to say, but then she nodded curtly and left them alone.

"Some more wine, Miss Trumble?" asked Robert.

"No, I thank you," said Miss Trumble, wanting to keep a clear head.

"Very well. Delighted as I am to have such an intelligent lady as my guest, I would like to know what brought you here. Has Jessica recovered from her ordeal?"

"I believe and I hope so."

He waited patiently and Miss Trumble said in an agonized voice, "I wish I knew how to put this without appearing impertinent. I have already taken a great deal too much upon myself for a lady of my station."

"Miss Trumble, I always get the feeling that somehow you are of a superior station in life to my own despite your profession. So let us just converse openly as equals."

Miss Trumble took a deep breath. "Jessica has changed. I always sensed she was a young lady of intelligence and character but ruined by the Beverley obsession to regain Mannerling. That obsession has gone and I know it will never return. But she is deeply unhappy—and because of you."

"Because of me?" he echoed. "I think I may consider myself the injured party in this, Miss Trumble."

"I believe Jessica did not know she was in love with you when she was here at Tarrant Hall. She now does, and that is what is making her unhappy, because she sees no hope for her and is now well aware of what she has thrown away."

A flush mounted to his face, but he said sharply, "You are a commendable governess and behave more like a mother to those girls than Lady Beverley. Therefore it is understandable that you should try to seek out marriageable gentlemen for them."

"I would not trick you, Mr. Sommerville," said Miss Trumble earnestly.

"But I am under the impression that this is all speculation. Jessica has said nothing to you?"

"No, but she looks so sad and she keeps talking in a longing kind of way of her visit here."

"I admit that I was on the point of proposing marriage to Jessica," he said. "But her feelings for me had no roots, there was no strong attachment there, for she hurried off home as soon as she learned through my own sister's machinations that there was still a chance of catching Harry Devers. I am sorry she suffered so badly at his hands, but I warned her against him . . . twice. If she had any respect for me or my feelings, she would not have treated me thus. I shall ensure that your stay here is pleasant, Miss Trumble, but we will not speak of this matter again. Look at it logically."

"I do not think that love has anything to do with logic," said Miss Trumble, but she felt defeated. "But perhaps there is a certain piece of logic you might consider. You can be in the right and miserable, or you can forgive and be happy. For myself, I think it is so much more pleasant to be happy."

Miss Trumble stayed a further two days, during which time neither Jessica's name nor that of any of the other Beverleys was mentioned. Although she had been urged to stay as long as she liked, she felt low, felt she was now there under false pretences. She had failed.

When she took her leave and shook hands with Robert and thanked him for his hospitality, she looked up anxiously into his face, but it was a well-bred mask.

Barry climbed into the post-chaise beside her. Robert had offered his own carriage, but Miss Trumble had declined. She had pointed out that if Lady Beverley found out where she and Barry had really been, both would lose their jobs.

Barry and she sat in silence as their carriage moved off.

"I gather from your downcast looks, miss," said Barry sympathetically, "that you did not achieve your aim."

"No, Barry, the damage has been done and there is no turning back. I feel like an old fool."

"Oh, never say that, miss. At least we tried. The gossip among the servants is all about how sad and miserable Mr. Robert is and how they hope he does not leave Tarrant Hall, for he is accounted a good master."

"How depressing it is to travel without hope," said Miss Trumble, half to herself.

"Things often work out the way they are meant to be," said Barry. "You cannot expect Mr. Robert to marry a girl he don't want, can you?"

"But he *must* want her." Miss Trumble sounded exasperated. "He is miserable, she is miserable, and the reason is they are both in love with each other. What a waste! All ruined because of one girl's folly and one man's stupid pride!"

Miss Trumble's spirits were cheered by the welcome she received from everybody when she finally returned to Brookfield House. She had stayed a night at the Green Man while Barry walked home on foot. Lady Beverley had been prey to severe headaches and there had been no Miss Trumble to soothe them away. Jessica longed to talk of Robert, however obliquely, and knew that Miss Trumble was her one sympathetic listener. Her sisters had come to realize how much they relied on Miss Trumble's help in all sorts of ways and all had admitted with surprise during her absence that they had also found the days long and dreary without lessons.

Miss Trumble was pressed to give a description of her visit to her fictitious relatives and felt guilty about lying. Barry had presented a fine selection of game to Lady Beverley, some of which Robert had supplied and some which Miss Trumble had bought from a dealer on the road home.

All the while she considered whether she should tell Jessica and only Jessica the truth of where she had been, for the sooner the girl lost any hope of ever seeing Robert Sommerville again, the sooner she could settle down and begin a new life, without Mannerling, without Robert.

But she had almost given up any idea of telling Jessica the truth until two days later, when Jessica came to her bedroom late at night. "Are you very sleepy?" asked Jessica. "I wish to talk."

"I am not sleepy," said Miss Trumble. "What would you like to talk about?"

"I had hoped," said Jessica, "that perhaps Mr. Robert might have forgiven me, might have written to me or called. I often wonder whether he found a new property or whether he is still at Tarrant Hall."

Miss Trumble became determined then to tell some of the truth. "I have seen Mr. Sommerville," she said and her heart sank at the blaze of hope that illumined Jessica's face. "Tarrant Hall lay on my way home, and so I made a brief call."

"Did he ask about me?"

"He hopes you are well."

"Did he say anything about calling on us?"

Miss Trumble reached forward and took Jessica's hand in a firm clasp.

"I am sorry, my dear, but he has set his heart against you. He feels he was treated shabbily. I am afraid he will not forgive you."

The light went out of Jessica's face. "So that is that," she said. "What a fool I was!"

"I trust Harry Devers has not come calling?"

"He would not dare. No, the gossips say his father has forced him to return to the army and so he has left Mannerling. Should I write to Mr. Sommerville? I never really apologized to him properly."

"I do not think so. It is better you forget about him, Jessica. If you wrote to him, you would go on in hope, hoping your letter would soften his heart, watching the post for a reply. Time will let you forget this whole sorry affair. I had hoped to bring you better news."

"No doubt Honoria makes sure that he does not forget," said Jessica bitterly.

"I am afraid you can no longer even blame Honoria. Her brother has been very low in spirits and I think she blames herself for that. She was kindness itself to me. At first I was suspicious of her, but she asked after you in such a kind way. Then she did not mention your name again, but that was because of Robert."

Jessica thanked her and said good night and went to her own room and sat down listlessly on the bed. Now there was no hope. Sad as she had been, she had continued to hope for a letter or to see the sight of his tall figure riding up the drive. Then she found it shocking that she should grieve so badly over the loss of Robert, as she had not grieved over the death of her own father. She felt God was punishing her for being such a silly and selfish fool.

She undressed and went to bed and lay awake a long time, dreading the arrival of a new day that would bring no hope of ever seeing Robert Sommerville again.

The following day was unusually mild for winter. Blue skies stretched over the bare branches of the trees and the bare brown earth of the fields. Jessica put on a warm wool gown and cloak, pattens, and wound a thick scarf around her head and set out for a long walk. She did not tell her mother or Miss Trumble because they would have insisted that Barry go with her, and Jessica wanted to be alone.

She came to a small hill. To the east of her lay Brookfield House, and to the west, Mannerling–Mannerling, source of all her troubles. The sun shone down palely, turning the puddles to gold and creating the false illusion of spring.

The hill also commanded a good view of the long road to Hedgefield. As she looked, she saw a tall figure on horseback riding along that road. How bitter it was to remember the times she had stood on this very hill, expecting every horseman in sight to be Robert Sommerville.

And then she stood very still, her heart beginning to beat hard. For as the rider came ever nearer, there was something familiar about that tall figure. Telling herself that her imagination was playing tricks with her eyes, she nonetheless began to run towards the road, stumbling every now and then as the high iron hoops on her pattens caught in a rut. She gained the road and leaned on a gate.

It *was* Robert, but the quick surge of gladness in her heart suddenly left, leaving her feeling cold. This road also led to Mannerling, and that must be where he was going. She wanted to draw back and hide, but he had seen her. He reined in his horse and dismounted and then stood on the other side of the gate looking down at her.

"Miss Jessica. Good day to you." He removed his hat and made her a low bow. His black hair gleamed in the sunlight.

All the flirtatious things that Jessica had planned to say in her imagination during the long days when she had thought of him disappeared from her mind and she cried out, "Oh, Mr. Sommerville, Mr. Sommerville, I am so very sorry. I have missed you so dreadfully. I have been such a silly fool. I know you do not want to have anything to do with me again, but only say that you will forgive me."

He stared at her in amazement and then, with a stifled exclamation, he lifted her clear over the gate and then gathered her into his arms and kissed her fiercely. The passion from the lips under his sent his senses reeling. His kisses were becoming deeper, and quite savage, and he had a sudden fear that he was behaving like Harry and that she would flee from him. He drew back a little but she buried her hands in his hair at the nape of his neck and drew his mouth back down to her own. They kissed and kissed with a single-minded intensity. Slowly the sun went down and a chill little wind began to blow.

Barry, who had been sent out to look for Jessica, came along the road waving a lantern. He saw the passionately entwined couple and stopped stock-still and then turned on his heel and scurried back as fast as he could in the direction of Brookfield House. He was met by Miss Trumble, who had come out to join in the search.

"Oh, miss!" cried Barry. "They're together, Mr. Robert and Miss Jessica, and they're kissing each other."

Miss Trumble smiled. "As a correct governess, I should go there and stop them. But . . . I think, I really think, that I am going to turn about and go home."

"Good idea," said Barry with a grin. "We won after all!"

"Did you find Jessica?" Lady Beverley was standing on the doorstep peering out into the night.

"Yes, my lady," said Miss Trumble.

"Then why is she not with you?"

"Jessica is with Mr. Robert Sommerville. I believe she met him on the Hedgefield road."

"Then she should be chaperoned. It is time I talked to you most severely about your duties here, Miss Trumble. You are only a governess and you take too much upon yourself."

To her irritation, Miss Trumble did not apologize or protest but stood quietly there holding a lantern. A bobbing light behind her headed towards the corner of the house and disappeared around it. "And that is no doubt Barry returned, and without reporting to me!" exclaimed Lady Beverley. "Ah, when I was at Mannerling, no servant would dare behave in such a way."

"I think that is them returning now," said Miss Trumble, hearing the clop of a horse's hooves on the road. She edged past her mistress and went into the house.

Robert, leading his horse with one hand and holding Jessica with the other, came up the drive.

"A word with you in private, Lady Beverley, if you please." Before Lady Beverley's shocked eyes, he kissed Jessica on the mouth. Barry appeared and took his horse round to the stable.

Lady Beverley led the way into the parlour. She dismissed her other daughters and then said, "I hope you can explain your behaviour, Mr. Sommerville."

"Easily, ma'am. I wish to marry Jessica."

Lady Beverley half-closed her eyes and then turned away and stared into the fire. Unknown to Jessica and the others, she had called on Mrs. Devers, and between them the two women had reknitted Harry's character into that of an endearing lost boy who only needed a good wife to put him right. That Lady Beverley should even contemplate such as Harry as a son-in-law would have been shocking to anyone but Mrs. Devers, whose heart had been made fonder by her son's absence. Lady Beverley thought it was like some kind of cruel torture the way her hopes kept being raised only to be dashed again.

She said wearily, "I suppose there is no stopping you."

Robert looked at her with a certain haughty pride. He was accustomed to thinking of himself as a good catch.

Lady Beverley saw the look on his face. "Sit down," she said. "We have business to discuss." If Robert Sommerville wanted Jessica, thought Lady Beverley grimly, then he should pay for it. She entered into a long discussion about marriage settlements, which put her in a high good humour, while Robert privately hoped that once he was married he would need to see as little of his mother-in-law as possible.

At last the ordeal was over. There was no champagne to celebrate this betrothal. Jessica looked radiantly happy, and only Rachel and Abigail thought her a fool. One day Harry would return on leave and that day would bring a return of their hopes to regain Mannerling.

* * *

And so Jessica and Robert were married, Jessica proudly wearing Isabella's wedding gown, and in her happiness and radiance making it look as if it had been made especially for her. Isabella had failed to make the journey. The weather had been too bad to make the crossing from Ireland, and she was reported to be still weak after the difficult birth of a son. Miss Trumble found herself silently praying throughout the wedding service for the future happiness of the other Beverley sisters. Lizzie was so delighted with the wedding that Miss Trumble had no fears about her. But she was doubtful about the others. Some of their old secrecy had returned. Honoria had been forgiven by Lizzie, and Honoria, so relieved and happy that she was to stay at Tarrant Hall after the marriage, had decided that Jessica was the best of girls.

There was dancing after the wedding breakfast, which was held in the Green Man in Hedgefield, Brookfield House having been considered too small by Lady Beverley, who was still furious with Jessica for having turned down the Deverses' kind offer to be married from Mannerling.

"Just look at them!" said the twins to Belinda as Robert and Jessica waltzed in each other's arms. "How mawkish."

"What can you mean?" exclaimed Belinda. "Only see how happy they are."

"Harry Devers could have been managed," said Abigail sulkily. "A woman can always manage a man."

"And what would you know of that?" jeered Belinda. But as the twins moved away, she began to wonder uneasily if Jessica had been too weak. "What are you thinking about?" asked Miss Trumble, popping up beside her.

"I was wondering whether Abigail spoke the truth, whether she had the right of it. She said that Jessica could have managed Harry Devers."

Miss Trumble took a deep breath. "Stop it now, Belinda. This is madness. Your poor sister was assaulted in the most frightening way and could, who knows, have been killed, and yet you say such as Harry Devers could have been *managed.* Fie for shame!"

"Oh, well," said Belinda. "I know nothing yet of men. But I shall."

And God prevent that day until you come to your senses, thought Miss Trumble.

On their wedding night, Robert and Jessica stopped at a posting-house on the road to Tarrant Hall. They were both silent and nervous, until Jessica said, "Robert, dear, I feel I am not yet ready for the intimacies of marriage. I am very fatigued. Perhaps we could wait a little . . . ?" Robert looked at her, his face rigid with disappointment. "As you will," he said. "But I only reserved the one bedchamber. Never mind, I will sleep on that chair over there."

Jessica was at first relieved. She undressed behind the bed-hangings and climbed into the high bed and tried to compose herself for sleep. The wind whistled outside and a branch tap-tap-tapped against the window.

"Robert," she said timidly, "are you comfortable?"

"No," came the reply.

"Oh." Jessica began to feel guilty. She had expected a few kisses and endearments. Not this brooding silence that fell on the room again after that short exchange. He did not understand her fears. She must try to explain. She climbed down from the bed and went round and stood in front of him. She was wearing a white muslin night-gown trimmed with lace. On her head was a ridiculous little lace nightcap. Her auburn hair lay on her shoulders.

"Robert," she pleaded, "do not be angry with me."

"I am not angry, my heart, but disappointed."

"All I beg of you is a little time. Please kiss me, Robert, before I go to sleep."

He stood up, still fully dressed in his wedding clothes, and kissed her chastely on the forehead.

"A proper kiss, please, Robert."

He tried to kiss her briefly on the mouth, but her lips clung to his own and the pair plunged into a vortex of passion that somehow ended up with both of them naked on the floor in front of the fire, with Jessica only being dimly aware of how they had got there. After some time, after she had lost her virginity in a mixture of pain and ecstasy, Robert said plaintively, "I think we would be better off in bed. Unless you are still frightened?"

"Oh, no, darling, and it would be more respectable, I think. What if some servant should come in and find us like this?"

"Then let us be respectable by all means, my love." He lifted her up in his arms and carried her to the bed.

Mrs. Devers awoke with a start during the night. As she lay in the darkness, she heard an odd tinkling sound. She got out of bed and put on her wrapper. Her husband's bedchamber was at the other end of the corridor, but she decided a tinkling noise was not very threatening. She followed the sound and came to the landing overlooking the great hall.

The Waterford crystal chandelier was slowly turning. It would turn half a circle and then turn back and the crystals tinkled. In sudden fear, she stared at the chandelier, which was on a level with her eyes. Judd, the previous owner, had hanged himself from that very chandelier. The chandelier was not lit, but by the dim light of one oil-lamp in the hall below and the light from another on the landing behind her, she could see the sparkle of the crystals. Then a log fell in the fire in the hall, and a red flame shot up. It seemed to Mrs. Devers's terrified eyes that in that red glow she could see a body hanging from the chandelier, revolving first in one half-circle, then back the other way, another half-circle. She put back her head and screamed and screamed until her husband and the servants came running. She could not tell them what had frightened her, only babble mindlessly. The doctor was summoned and prescribed rest and a change of scene.

It was only when they were on the road to Brighton that Mrs. Devers recovered her powers of speech. Her husband patted her hand after she had stumbled out that she had seen Ajax Judd hanging from the chandelier. "It was a windy night," he said. "The oil-lamps were flickering and throwing weird shadows."

"It's that house," wailed Mrs. Devers. "It will kill us as it killed Judd."

"How can a house kill anyone? Give your mistress some laudanum," Mr. Devers said to the maid seated opposite. "She becomes agitated again."

Mrs. Devers soon sank into a laudanum-induced sleep and the carriage rolled ever forward to Brighton, and as the miles separated the Deverses from Mannerling, so did Mrs. Devers begin to recover her full sanity and her spirits.

For the moment, Mannerling was forgotten.

Chapter Ten

I only took the regular course . . . the different branches of Arithmetic—Ambition, Distraction, Uglification and Derision.

—LEWIS CARROLL

Now they were four—the four Beverley sisters, not six any more. They had been proudly aware of the effect of their combined beauty when there had been six of them and felt diminished, and Belinda, Rachel, and Abigail privately thought that Lizzie did not really count, being damned with red hair.

Miss Trumble kept them at their lessons, finding the sisters subdued and biddable. It was as if the sisters had recovered from a madness and yet without it, felt their days quiet and without ambition.

Rachel and Abigail, the twins, both attained their nineteenth birthdays, well aware that there would be no coming-out for either of them. Rachel quietly accepted this state of affairs, but Abigail could not help hoping that either Isabella or Jessica might decide to take a house in London and present them.

The twins were very alike in appearance, both with large blue eyes and fair, curly hair. But Rachel's eyes held a dreamy look, whereas Abigail's were usually alive with either frustration or anger. Although she privately agreed that plotting and scheming to get back to Mannerling had been a ridiculous and childish way to go on, she could not help thinking of the days when her birthday would be marked with a present of jewelry from her parents and a grand party.

At last, she sat down and wrote to Jessica, hinting broadly what fun it would be to go to London and how flat and dreary life in the country was with no beaux and nothing but lessons to enlive the tedium of the days.

"I am going to Hedgefield," said Miss Trumble when she had finished the morning's schooling, "and will be happy to take any letters you might have to the mail coach."

Abigail slid that precious letter from under her mathematics primer. "I have one here for Jessica," she said. "We have not heard from her this age."

Miss Trumble looked surprised. "Jessica wrote every week when she was on her honeymoon and now she is returned, she still writes regularly. Lady Beverley read you out loud her latest letter at dinner last night."

"I forgot," mumbled Abigail who had meant that a proper letter never arrived, by which she meant one suggesting a London Season.

"Will she invite us all to visit her?" asked Lizzie eagerly.

"Perhaps soon," said Miss Trumble, but casting a sharp look at Abigail. "They will wish to get settled in and accustomed to the married state. Perhaps in the summer. The roads are too bad for travel at the moment."

Abigail handed her the sealed letter and Miss Trumble weighed it thoughtfully in her hand, looking down at it as if wishing she could read what was inside.

But she merely nodded to them all and left the room. "What were you writing to Jessica about?" asked Rachel. "We all sent a joint letter only last week."

"I hinted–only hinted, mind you," said Abigail, "that it might be fun to go to London."

"London!" exclaimed Rachel. "Why London?"

"Because that's where we should be making our come-out. Robert Sommerville could well afford to take a town house."

"I do not think he will do that," said Lizzie, resting her

pointed chin on her hand. "He is so scholarly and thinks a life between university and home enough for him. Besides, perhaps he thinks we are a bad influence."

"Us? Why?" asked Belinda.

"Because of Mannerling. Perhaps he might think we will talk of Mannerling again."

"Oh, we would never do that!" said Rachel. "We have learned our lesson."

"We'll see," said Abigail firmly. Now that the letter had gone, she felt that a London Season was only a matter of time. And it was London, not Mannerling.

Miss Trumble, being driven to Hedgefield by Barry, said, "I have a letter to post. It is from Abigail to Mrs. Sommerville."

"You do seem worried about it," said Barry, glancing sideways at her. "What is there to worry about in a letter from one sister to another?"

"I suppose I must be reassured that Jessica never thinks of Mannerling now that she is married and so much in love. For I believe that Abigail might still harbour ambitions. And there is something secretive about the girls. They are friendly towards me and yet somehow they hold me at bay."

"Little Miss Lizzie led me to believe that they were feeling ashamed of themselves for having encouraged Miss Jessica to have anything to do with Harry Devers," said Barry. "Could be, they really are a bit ashamed of themselves."

"I wonder. But I must prevail on Lady Beverley to allow me to arrange some balls and local assemblies for the girls to attend. Ever since Jessica's marriage, she has left them to me and takes no interest in her own daughters! There are plenty of eligible young men in the county. Lady Beverley should be going on calls, renewing the acquaintance with mothers of marriageable sons.

"I feel at times that I have all the burdens of a parent without the power or privileges."

"And yet," said Barry with a sly look at her, "I feel you've had power and privilege at one time."

"Ruling a schoolroom gives one a certain arrogance," said Miss Trumble vaguely. "Well, here is Hedgefield. I must post this letter and pray that Abigail is not up to any mischief."

Jessica, Mrs. Sommerville, read Abigail's letter several times, a frown on her pretty face. She and her husband were at Tarrant Hall and Honoria was still in residence, an Honoria so grateful that Jessica had not turned her out, that she had become a friend instead of an enemy.

"Not bad news?" asked Robert from the other side of the breakfast table.

"It is from Abigail."

"The twin?"

"Yes. She hints that she would love to go to London. She says her birthday was monstrous flat and that it is such a pity she cannot make her come-out."

"By which she means that you should take a house in London and bring her out?"

"Yes, I suppose that is exactly what she means."

"So what do you feel about that, my love? I am quite happy to fund you."

"Robert, I can only remember with shame my cruelty to you and my silly ambition. I would not wish any of my sisters to suffer the same thing. If I could persuade myself that they had given up hopes of Mannerling, I would gladly bring out both Rachel and Abigail. If they still have ambitions in that direction, then they will go to London, determined only to find the richest man possible. I do not know what to do."

"Write and suggest they come to us later in the year when the weather is better and the roads safe for travel. That way, you can make up your mind."

"Oh, thank you, Robert. You are so good to me, I don't know how I can ever repay you."

He rose and went round the table and lifted her straight

up out of her chair and cradled her in his arms. He bent his mouth to hers and kissed her long and deep. Then he smiled down into her eyes and said softly, "Like this."

Abigail had run out every day to meet the post boy, always looking for that precious reply. London! She could hardly pay attention to her lessons. Her mind was in the ballroom. She was aware of Miss Trumble's shrewd eyes on her but she did not care. It would soon be goodbye to Miss Trumble. Let her stay behind and school Belinda and Lizzie! Never for a moment did Abigail think of appealing to her mother. Lady Beverley moved through her days in a vague dream, only rousing herself to get out the account books when Mr. Ducket, her husband's former secretary, came on a visit.

And then one frosty morning, the letter arrived. Abigail snatched it out of the post bag and shot up to her room. With trembling fingers, she broke the seal and scanned the contents. She could hardly believe what she was reading. No mention of glorious London. Trivia about Tarrant Hall and a suggestion that they should all come on a long visit in the summer and perhaps attend local balls and parties.

Angry tears filled Abigail's blue eyes. It was too bad of Jessica. So thoughtless! So uncaring!

And then she thought of Isabella. And this time she would not hint. She would state her desires in broad terms.

Isabella, Lady Fitzpatrick was at her home in Ireland. She and her husband had been staying with friends in a neighbouring county and so it was a week after Abigail's letter arrived that she sat down to read it.

"Faith, my love," she said to her husband. "Here's a coil. Abigail wishes me to take a house in London and present her. She says if I do not do so, I will be the most selfish person in the world."

Lord Fitzpatrick surveyed his wife. "Does Abigail know that you are expecting our second child?"

"I can only assume it has slipped her memory. Dear me! Such an *angry* letter. She says she is so bored and unhappy. Why does she not apply to mama? You have sent mama so much money since we were married."

"Perhaps she has taken up gambling like her late husband?"

"God forbid! I know. I shall write to Barry Wort and ask him what is really going on at home. Mama could well afford by now to take a house for the Season. And Jessica wrote to me to say that Robert had sent her very generous sums of money."

"I do not know that we can begin to question Lady Beverley about what she has done with our gifts. Write to Barry by all means."

"And what shall I write to Abigail?"

"She is obviously bored and restless. Suggest that she and her twin come here for a stay. Plenty of young men to keep them amused."

Abigail, on receiving this second rejection, did not rage or fume. She accepted it with a sad dignity. She felt she was being punished for being too vain and wordly. The weather had improved.

She decided to settle down and attend to her studies. She did not want to go to Ireland. She felt ashamed now of her demands. Her sisters appeared happy and content because they had accepted their situation.

Miss Trumble accepted this new and changed Abigail with relief. She decided it was time to broach the subject of balls and parties for them. Lady Beverley must do something. But Lady Beverley when appealed to exclaimed at the expense that would incur. "They will be demanding new gowns," she complained. "We must economise."

In vain did the governess protest and say that she would make over their gowns, that she herself would take the girls on calls to neighbouring households. "I am busy," Lady

Beverley replied curtly. "Go away. You are hired to school the girls, and so I suggest you go about it."

Miss Trumble was just turning away, defeated, when she saw Barry signalling to her outside the parlour window. She went outside and joined him.

"Walk around the back of the house with me," urged Barry. "I have strange news."

Wondering, Miss Trumble walked with him to the pleasant-smelling kitchen garden. Barry pulled a letter out of his coat. "This here is from Miss Isabella, I mean Lady Fitzpatrick. Do but read it."

Miss Trumble read the letter carefully and then looked at Barry in amazement. "According to this, Lady Beverley should have plenty of money and yet we all have to scrimp and save. Why is she hoarding it? What for?"

"I reckon," said Barry heavily, "that the lady may have incurred debts she is not talking about."

"Lady Beverley," said Miss Trumble, tapping the letter impatiently, "discusses every debt from the butcher to the baker to the candlestickmaker, loudly and often. She would not keep anything back. Unless . . ."

"Unless what, miss?"

"Mannerling! Lady Beverley has been closeted with that Mr. Ducket. He has probably been investing it for her, turning money into more money."

"What has that to do with Mannerling?"

"Don't you see? She wants to buy it back!"

"But it would take years to accumulate enough."

"Lady Beverley is mad enough to think she can do it. I'll swear that is the case. We have work to do, Barry. I shall defeat that wretched house if it is the last thing I do! I'll make Lady Beverley loose the purse strings. My girls shall not be made to suffer."

The Beverley sisters had, thought Barry sadly, indeed become Miss Trumble's girls, for their own mother appeared to have forgotten their very existence.